THE LEGACY SERIES

AF097795

SERIES TITLES

All That It Seems
Jim Landwehr

I Felt My Life With Both My Hands
Jessica Treadway

Hands
Pardeep Toor

Lafferty, Looking for Love
Dennis McFadden

This Is How We Speak
Rebecca Reynolds

All Gone Now
Michael Tasker

Your Place in This World
Jake La Botz

Apple & Palm
Patricia Henley

Bodies in Bags
Jamey Gallagher

A Green Glow on the Horizon
Dawn Burns

How We Do Things Here
Matt Cashion

Neon Steel
Jennifer Maritza McCauley

Release of Information
Kali White VanBaale

The Divide
Evan Morgan Williams

Yes, No, I Don't Know
Kathryn Gahl

The Price of Their Toys
John Loonam

The Caged Man
Calvin Mills

A Day Doesn't Go By When I Don't Have Regrets
J. Malcolm Garcia

These Are My People
Steve Fox

We Should Be Somewhere by Now
Stephen Tuttle

Burner and Other Stories
Katrina Denza

The Plan of Chicago
Barry Pearce

Trust Issues
K.P. Davis

Adult Children
Laurence Klavan

Guardians & Saints
Diane Josefowicz

Western Terminus: Stories and A Novella
Michael Keefe

Like Human
Janet Goldberg

The Hopefuls
Elizabeth Oness

Never Stop Exiting
Michael Hopkins

Broken Heart Syndrome
Anne Colwell

The Mexican Messiah: A Novella & Stories
Jay Kauffmann

Close to a Flame
Colleen Alles

American Animism
Jamey Gallagher

Keeping What's Best Left Kept Secret
David Ricchiute

Soaked
Toby LeBlanc

The Path of Totality
Marie Zhuikov

Shocker in Gloomtown
Dan Libman

The Continental Divide
Bob Johnson

The Three Devils and Other Stories
William Luvaas

The Correct Response
Manfred Gabriel

Welcome Back to the World: A Novella & Stories
Rob Davidson

Greyhound Cowboy and Other Stories
Ken Post

Close Call
Kim Suhr

The Waterman
Gary Schanbacher

Signs of the Imminent Apocalypse and Other Stories
Heidi Bell

What We Might Become
Sara Reish Desmond

The Silver State Stories
Michael Darcher

An Instinct for Movement
Michael Mattes

The Machine We Trust
Tim Conrad

Gridlock
Brett Biebel

Salt Folk
Ryan Habermeyer

The Commission of Inquiry
Patrick Nevins

Maximum Speed
Kevin Clouther

Reach Her in This Light
Jane Curtis

The Spirit in My Shoes
John Michael Cummings

The Effects of Urban Renewal on Mid-Century America and Other Crime Stories
Jeff Esterholm

What Makes You Think You're Supposed to Feel Better
Jody Hobbs Hesler

Fugitive Daydreams
Leah McCormack

Hoist House: A Novella & Stories
Jenny Robertson

Finding the Bones: Stories & A Novella
Nikki Kallioy

Self-Defense
Corey Mertes

Where Are Your People From?
James B. De Monte

Sometimes Creek
Steve Fox

The Plagues
Joe Baumann

The Clayfields
Elise Gregory

Kind of Blue
Christopher Chambers

Evangelina Everyday
Dawn Burns

Township
Jamie Lyn Smith

Responsible Adults
Patricia Ann McNair

Great Escapes from Detroit
Joseph O'Malley

Nothing to Lose
Kim Suhr

The Appointed Hour
Susanne Davis

PRAISE FOR
All That It Seems

The stories in *All That It Seems* are brimming with life, humor and heartbreak. Jim Landwehr has a brilliant eye for the details and dialogue that make the worlds he's created, and his characters, jump to life on the page.

—FRANK BURES
author of *Pushing the River*

All That It Seems is a smorgasbord of enchanting short stories that left me anxious for the next course. The stories were at times lighthearted and amusing and at other times deeply moving. There were jaw-dropping endings, laugh-out-loud scenes, and stories that touched my heart. Landwehr is a master storyteller.

—GREGORY LEE RENZ
author of *Beyond the Flames*

Jim Landwehr takes a humorous poke at contemporary culture in this short story collection. Lots of laugh-out-loud moments with underlying themes that made me go, hmmm.

—NANCI RATHBUN
author of the *Angelina Bonaparte* mysteries

Delightful and imaginative, Landwehr's inventive and clever stories settle into the nooks of our humanity, where they prickle and gnaw at our impulse, desire, and restraint.

—STEVE FOX
author *These Are My People*

Jim Landwehr skillfully combines warmth, humor, mystery, surprise, and social commentary in this engaging collection. You won't want to stop reading *All That It Seems*, and once you're done, you'll find yourself returning to it again and again.

—NICK CHIARKAS
author of *Nunzio's Way*

All That It Seems is a rich collection of short stories that explore life's tensions and connections. Grounded in the Midwest, Landwehr deftly handles themes ranging from aging and acceptance to stereotyping and AI. Each story is rich with emotional resonance—sometimes humorous, sometimes magical, always insightful.

—NANCY JORGENSEN
co-author of *Go, Gwen, Go*

Jim Landwehr is a writer you can trust. In prose tight as a new thread, he offers insight into the closely held beliefs modern man uses to navigate life and deal with the human condition. Tongue-in-cheek observations will make you chuckle. Clever twists will give you pause. Landwehr has crafted a narrative dripping with irony that stands popular memes on their ears. This great-hearted storyteller challenges the reader to look beyond the cliched notions that guide our behavior and belief. He nudges the reader toward that "ah ha" moment, at once surprising and satisfying. Eventually, you will be guided back to your easy chair, amused and content in the knowledge you have explored the path not often taken, stardust in your eyes.

—ROBERT GOSWITZ
author of *The Dragon Soldier's Good Fortune*

ALL THAT IT SEEMS

stories

JIM LANDWEHR

CORNERSTONE PRESS
UNIVERSITY OF WISCONSIN-STEVENS POINT

Cornerstone Press, Stevens Point, Wisconsin 54481
Copyright © 2026 Jim Landwehr
www.uwsp.edu/cornerstone

Printed in the United States of America.

Library of Congress Control Number: 2026932258
ISBN: 978-1-968148-42-3

All rights reserved.

This is a work of fiction. Names, characters, businesses, places, events, and incidents are either the products of the author's imagination or used in a fictitious manner. Any resemblance to actual persons, living or dead, or actual events is purely coincidental.

Cornerstone Press titles are produced in courses and internships offered by the Department of English at the University of Wisconsin–Stevens Point.

DIRECTOR & PUBLISHER	EXECUTIVE EDITORS
Dr. Ross K. Tangedal	Jeff Snowbarger, Freesia McKee
EDITORIAL DIRECTOR	SENIOR EDITORS
Brett Hill	Paige Biever, Ellie Atkinson, Lhea Owens

PRESS STAFF
Samantha Bjork, Sophie McPherson, Eleanor Belcher, Christina Niedzwiecki, Asher Schroeder, Andrew Bryant

*To my wife, Donna,
and our two children, Sarah and Benjamin,
all of whom are voracious readers. Our family's collective love
of the written word warms my heart.*

ALSO BY JIM LANDWEHR:

Nonfiction
At the Lake
Cretin Boy
The Portland House: A '70s Memoir
Dirty Shirt: A Boundary Waters Memoir

Poetry
Tea in the Pacific Northwest
Thoughts from a Line at the DMV
Genetically Speaking: Poems on Fatherhood
On a Road
Reciting From Memory
Written Life

stories

The Mayor of Pidgeon Ridge   1

All That It Seems   17

Divergence   27

Children of Mother Earth   42

Tea in the Pacific Northwest   55

Priceless   66

Ethangora   79

Fender Bender   85

The Brethren of Postocrity   103

Just What I Thought   110

A Cast of 10,000   126

Nightcall   136

Through These Eyes   143

Acknowledgments   159

The Mayor of Pidgeon Ridge

Kenneth held the hallowed iPad high over his head and banged the desk with his fist, signaling for quiet among the other residents.

"Order, everyone, order now!" he said.

A dozen seniors sat in chairs in a semicircle and another five in wheelchairs, listening with varying levels of cognition and interest. Marie had dozed off twenty minutes earlier, as she was known to do every couple of hours, a characteristic that earned her the title of "Sleepy." Lou, who was eighty-five, cupped his ear to hear better, having lost his hearing aids a month ago. He's unsure but thinks they may have gone through the kitchen garbage disposal when he'd taken them off at dinner and put them under a napkin. Either that or someone had stolen them.

"Damn you, Kenneth!" Francine shouted from her wheelchair. "Damn you to hell!"

Kenneth lowered the iPad. "Now that's enough, Francine! No more of that. We have business to conduct here," Kenneth replied.

"Business? What business?" Jack said from his spot on the couch. "And who made you the mayor of Pigeon Ridge, anyway?"

Jack was a silver-haired, handsome devil. He'd arrived at the center a few weeks before the pandemic and proved to be a romantic hit among the ladies at Pigeon Ridge Senior Center. Tall and athletic for his seventy-three years, he'd played quarterback for a handful of years for the Calgary Stampede. Jack spent a little time on the practice squad for the Detroit Lions but never quite made it to the big time. His appeal lay in his genuineness as much as his looks. When he talked to people, he listened intently, asked questions, and leaned in when his interest was piqued. When he came to Pigeon Ridge, these qualities caused quite a stir among the women and a fair amount of jealousy in a few male residents, especially Kenneth, who was older and required a walker to get around.

"I was elected, for your information. It was a vote, fair and square. We voted at the start of the sickness; don't you remember?" Kenneth asked.

"No, frankly, I don't. And I wouldn't have voted for you, anyway. You're corrupt!"

The crowd let out a collective gasp at the accusation. A murmur swept over the residents, forcing Kenneth to raise the iPad high again and pound his fist to quiet the room. "People, people! I've got the iPad!" he shouted with authority. Quiet slowly returned to the room.

"Damn you, iPad Kenneth!" Francine shouted.

"Francine, if you don't stop, I'll have to have Stan the Enforcer forcibly remove you to serve some time in the closet of correction and shame." He looked to his right, where Stan sat with his cane in his lap. Stan moved a little slow, but he'd worked his life in the tree trimming business, so he was a big man.

"Do you understand me? The mayor deserves respect; otherwise, what you have is chaos, and chaos leads to death," Kenneth said.

"Death, please take me!" Shirley shouted from her wheelchair. Like Francine, she had her trademark catchphrase. In her case, it was the only phrase she ever uttered. Frankly,

Kenneth secretly wished her plea would be granted, as her outbursts were annoying and an unpleasant reminder of what they all faced, some sooner than others.

"Oh, Shirley, you're fine. Now, please, let's get down to business," Kenneth said. "Will the Board of Octogenarians please give their weekly status report?"

Dorothy slowly rose from her chair with her notebook in hand. "Well, since the last meeting, everything we've seen on the news says the pandemic is still spreading like wildfire throughout central Wisconsin. Furthermore, Pigeon Ridge staff is under a state order to continue to quarantine at home for at least another couple of weeks. That means no contact with us or this facility. Knowing these orders, we still collectively maintain the locked-door policy should remain in place for everyone here. Remember everyone, the infection is out *there*, not in here. This one's nothing to mess around with, and if it gets in here, we're all dead."

"Death, please take me!" Shirley exclaimed.

"Lighten up, Shirley," Dorothy said and continued with her report. "On the ration and supply side of things, our inventory shows someone has been stealing granola bars from the kitchen. There were about a dozen missing at last count, and as we all know, we can't have theft. Everyone gets equal."

"Well, someone stole a pair of scissors from my room last week," Arnie said accusingly.

"Did they leave a granola bar in its place?" Dorothy asked.

"Why, no, they didn't."

"Then what's your point? We were talking about the damn granola bars, not your scissors. Pardon my language, Mayor Kenneth."

The mayor nodded in her direction. "Please finish your report, Dorothy."

"Well, as long as we're discussing food, we got word from our provider that they can't get us more until next Thursday. The entire distribution network is in an awful state, especially the trucking industry. They're also not sure how transmissible the spores are, so all the food has to be quarantined for ten days before delivery. This is part of the reason Pigeon Ridge staff was told to stay away from this place until things calm down with the sickness. That said, from a meal perspective, things will be tight until the next delivery. So, given the latest granola bar scandal, this board recommends we vote on the startup of a 24/7 kitchen guard patrol. And finally, um, well, I can't read my handwriting for the last part of my report. Something about toilet paper, I think. So in lieu of a closing point, that about covers it."

"Damn you! And damn your toilet paper, too!" Francine added.

Mayor Kenneth gave Francine a side-eye but ignored her latest outburst. "I think this calls for a vote, then. All those in favor of establishing around-the-clock kitchen guard, please raise your hand."

All the residents raised their hands, except Jack.

Kenneth continued. "It appears we have a majority, so I would request the board to put together a list of volunteers to guard the kitchen. Also, I would like to know why you didn't raise your hand, Jack?"

"Because you're corrupt! Besides, it's a free country, isn't it?"

"Or maybe it's because a security detail might thwart your granola theft ring?" Dorothy accused.

"Damn you, granola thief!" Francine added, pointing at Jack.

"I don't even like granola!" Jack said defensively.

Kenneth spoke up, trying to restore order. "Okay, enough about the damn granola, already. So, we'll circulate a volunteer list for kitchen guard duty after the meeting. Please help where you can. Before I close the meeting, are there any comments from the community?"

Rose's hand shot into the air. Kenneth sighed deeply, then acknowledged her. "Rose?"

"Yeah, I want to know who made the lights out by 10 p.m. rule?"

"That was something I did of my own accord, thinking it was best that everyone gets a good night's sleep," Kenneth replied.

"What? You're not the boss of us! Last night, Watchman Willie came by and made me turn out my lights. Next time I'll stay up until I'm good and ready to go to sleep!" Rose declared.

"Damn you, dream police!" Francine shouted.

Rose had been Mayor Kenneth's biggest enemy ever since his election seven days ago. Before the global pandemic, the two of them had been in a screaming match when she saw him walking without his walker and called him out on it.

"I'm fine. Mind your own business, ya old crab," he'd said.

The insult led to Rose standing and getting nose-to-nose with Kenneth as they exchanged words. Eventually, the head attendant at the front desk stepped in, separated the two, and sent them back to their rooms. In the election a week prior, Rose had written in a vote for Jack because she couldn't bring herself to vote for Kenneth even though he ran unopposed. Ever since the virus closed the doors of the center, she'd spent her time trying to drum up support for Jack to take over as mayor. Every morning since, Kenneth had found a note on his door reading, "Impeach Mayor Kenneth. Vote for Jack!" He knew it had to be Rose. She held a mean grudge.

"Well, okay, we need a vote on the lights-out policy, then. Who thinks we should change it to, say, midnight?"

"You're just trying to cover up your abuse of power, Kenneth. Well, I ain't biting. You should be impeached!" Rose said.

"I'm sorry, did you say something, Rose? I was ignoring you. Now back to the vote. Should we change the lights-out policy to midnight?"

"Ha! I haven't seen midnight for twenty years! What do I care? I ain't voting," Jack said, standing and excusing himself.

The rest of the residents were left with raised hands. Kenneth waited a second and said, "Well, despite the outliers, it looks like we have a majority for the lights-out extension. Midnight it is. Party on. This meeting's adjourned unless there are any more comments."

"Death, please take me!"

Charlene and Laura sipped their cups of Keurig-brewed coffee and listened intently as Rose spoke from the closed-door confines of her room. She wore her usual lavender caftan with a daisy pattern near the neckline.

Rose took a sip of her coffee and said, "He's a snake, I tell you. I've never liked the guy since the day we met. He's an arrogant narcissist; I can tell. I wouldn't put it past him to be the culprit behind the missing granola bars. He's just that low. We need to strip him of his mayoral power, by whatever means necessary."

"Well, I've always thought he was a handsome fellow myself," Charlene said.

"Ew! No! I don't see it. He's got jowls for one thing," Laura added.

Rose spoke up again. "I'm with Laura, but to each their own. I can see right through his fake personality. The decision about lights-out was just an arrogant abuse of power. Who knows how long this virus is going to keep us secluded? We need to get him out, one way or the other. And you already know who has my support to replace him."

"Kenneth!" Laura said.

"What? No, *Jack*, Laura! Get it right. Jack," Rose corrected.

"Oh, right. I forgot what we were talking about. You know my memory isn't what it once was."

"I see that, but those two guys could not be more different, so be sure you get it right if we ever have a revolt. It's Jack. Jack's the good guy!"

"Jack. Got it. And he's the one stealing the granola bars, right?" Laura said.

"No, no, no. Jack's good, Kenneth's evil, and we don't know who's stealing granola."

"Oh, it's all just so much. I think I need a nap," Laura said with a yawn.

"It's not rocket surgery, Laura. There's only one name we support, remember? Jack!" Charlene added.

"So anyway, I'm organizing an Impeach Kenneth march for this Thursday. We're going to walk down to his door and read from my list of grievances. I intend to build support from the other residents by making a lot of noise along the way. I need to know you ladies are with me."

"Well, that sounds highly political, so count me in!" Laura said.

"Do you have any other supporters?" Charlene asked.

Rose set down her coffee and licked her lips. "I've talked to a couple of others—Michael, Sandy, and Carol. I think they're on board, but even with them, it would be a close vote, so I'm looking to win over a couple more instigators along the way. We'll just have to wait and see, I guess."

Laura chimed in. "Yep. Well, I have to go and take my afternoon meds and get my nap in."

"Alright, well just remember, Laura: Jack is good, Kenneth is bad," Rose said as a reminder.

"Okay, I think I've got it. But who's stealing the granola again?" Laura asked.

Pedro knocked on Walter's door and after a few seconds, it swung open. Walter stood there in sweatpants and a Packers sweatshirt. "Hey, what's up my friend?" he said.

Pedro quickly flashed a flask from his hoodie pocket and said, "Got time for a little treat and a chat, brother?"

Walter raised his eyebrows and stepped aside to let him in. Pedro walked over and moved the dirty laundry off the armchair next to Walter's recliner. He sat as Walter shuffled over to get a couple of rock glasses. Walter handed them to him and sat down in the recliner.

Pedro poured the amber whiskey into one glass and passed it to Walter, who asked, "So, what's up?"

Pedro poured himself a glass and began. "Well, what's up is I'm looking to bust out of this place."

Walter almost choked on his first sip of whiskey. "What? How do you propose to do that? With the virus raging like it is, leaving here would be a kiss of death. What are you thinking?"

"I'll be honest with you, friend, I've been borderline depressed for a few months now. I can't help but think about the hopelessness of my situation. What kind of life do I have in here? Same thing, day in and day out. Gossip around the TV, stupid adult crafts and games, and always, always, always chicken for dinner! There's a part of me that sees the adventure in busting out, and if anyone ever wanted to escape, now is the time. There are literally no care workers stopping us from doing anything. Frankly, at this point in my life, breaking out sounds freeing."

"Well, I think you're nuts. But I also agree life is a little redundant around here. How do you propose to get out?"

Pedro took a swig from his glass and flashed a whiskey-faced wince. "I figure Big Ed works the Thursday night security shift, and I know for a fact he sleeps through half of it. The guy is narcoleptic during day hours for cripes sake. While he's snoozing, I'll just snatch the key and slip on out the door."

"You always were a bit of a tortured soul, Pedro. I hope it works. I'll be anxious to check your room on Friday morning.

Cheers to the great escape!" Walter said, raising his glass. Pedro clinked it and they both took drinks.

The chants echoed down the fluorescent-lit hallway.
"Who is it that we want out?"
"Kenneth, Kenneth, Kenneth Stout!"
"What's he done to start this fight?"
"He makes us turn out the lights!"
The crowd of seniors walked slowly in a plodding procession. A couple of them brandished brooms, and Sandy Clarkson held a toilet brush aloft, shaking it at every door they passed like some sort of holy water blessing, sans the water. Michael Niebler banged a frying pan with a ladle in time to the chant. He'd taken both items from the industrial kitchen to give the uprising a musical emphasis. Mrs. Feldman wore a sandwich board made from an old pizza box held together by shoestrings. Written around the grease stains, it read:

> *He's no big cheese*
> *dump Kenneth Stout!*
> *Jack is the secret sauce*
> *we're all talking about!*

When the mob reached Leonard's room, they paused for about thirty seconds, chanting. It was common knowledge that he and Kenneth were best friends, and that Leonard was his most ardent supporter. Leonard came to the door wielding a crutch he'd used after he'd twisted his ankle during Chicken Dance Wednesday in the cafeteria a few weeks earlier. He held the crutch out like a fencing foil, jabbing it toward the crowd, shouting, "It's a free country. What do you want from me, anyway?"
"Damn your free country!" Francine shouted.
"We want your vote for Jack, Leonard," Rose said.
"Damn you, Jack Leonard!"

"Francine, it's not Jack Leonard. They're two separate people. Oh, never mind, and shut up!" Rose said.

"Well, you ain't gettin' it. Now get outta here and keep the noise down. I'm trying to take a nap," Leonard answered.

"Prepare for disappointment then, Leonard," Rose said belligerently. "Because he's going down."

Leonard slammed the door, and the small crowd of insurrectionists moved slowly down the hallway.

Pedro leaned hard against the hallway wall and peeked around the corner of the reception area. He wore jeans and a flannel shirt and was carrying a backpack stuffed with snacks and a change of clothes. It was a little past 11:30 p.m., and true to his prediction, Big Ed sat flopped back in his chair, mouth wide open, catching flies. Pedro crept over to the counter and scanned the desk. He saw a ring of keys hanging from a hook on the underside. Quietly reaching, he grabbed the ring and turned toward the door. As he did, the keys fell to the floor.

Big Ed roused and rubbed his face, looking around to see what had awakened him. Pedro had picked up the keys and was on his hands and knees in front of the reception desk, trying to stifle his panicked breathing. He stayed crouched for a couple of minutes before he heard the light snoring coming again from Big Ed. Pedro made his way to the door and started trying different keys in the lock. On the third try, the tumbler clicked, and Pedro slipped out. He had thirty-seven dollars in his wallet, and suddenly the whole world lay before him, pandemic be damned.

In the greeting area of the center, Kenneth raised the iPad and called the meeting to order. The residents were seated in front of him on sofas, chairs, and wheelchairs. Everyone, that was, except Rose, who remained standing in the back. She was wearing a white t-shirt with the words, "Impeach

Kenneth, NOW!" scrawled in black Sharpie marker across the front of it.

"Thank you for coming to this special session on such short notice. I want to start the meeting with the news many of you probably haven't heard yet. Our friend and fellow resident Pedro seems to have gone missing. Has anyone seen him since last night?" Kenneth asked.

A few residents gasped, but most just shook their heads and looked around.

"How'd he get out? Don't we have a door monitor?" Charlene asked, looking in Big Ed's direction.

"Well, it seems after we reviewed the closed-circuit video that Big Ed was sleeping at the time Pedro took the key and left. We found the key still in the lock this morning."

Big Ed shifted nervously in his seat as all eyes turned in his direction.

"Damn you, Big Ed!" Francine shouted.

"Calm down, everyone. The Board of Octogenarians met this morning and talked about the situation, and we've decided to look at his escape in a positive light. We concluded most of us were brought here against our wishes, so if a person wants out badly enough, they should be granted the privilege. Pedro's escape would never have been availed to him if we were fully staffed with care workers. We say, good for Pedro!"

Arnie was the first one to clap. His slow, methodical clapping triggered a second, then a third person to start applauding. Before long, the entire room was clapping and chanting, "Run, Pedro, run! Run, Pedro, run!"

After the room quieted, Rose raised her hand and blurted out, "Kenneth, before we begin, I'd like to make a motion we call for a special impeachment vote."

"Motion denied. Now be quiet, Rose. I have the hallowed iPad," Kenneth replied, raising it over his head. A chorus of boos came from many of the residents. Kenneth looked out in surprise. He hadn't expected to see such support for Rose and her cause.

"Yeah, Kenneth. We want a vote!" Jack hollered. A handful of other residents shouted their agreement.

"Rose, we're going to need a reason for any sort of impeachment vote. I hope you realize that," Dorothy said.

Rose lifted a sheet of paper over her head. "Oh, I have a list of grievances right here, Dorothy. Let me start with the obvious abuse of power in the lights-out policy. Then, there is the open meeting violation where none of us residents were informed that Pajama Fridays were being moved to Thursdays. You and the board just went ahead and changed it. Next, there's the unsolved granola bar thefts. Yes, I blame this on you. And finally, there's Pedro's great escape last night, which was during your tenure, I might add. In my opinion, since the beginning of our pandemic isolation here, Pigeon Ridge is going down the shitter, and I blame that squarely on you. I say, let the people vote and turn over the hallowed iPad to Jack to bring Pigeon Ridge back to its pre-pandemic glory."

"Hear, hear!" Charlene said.

"Death take me now!" Shirley exclaimed.

"Can it wait until after the vote, Shirley? We need your vote," Rose added snidely.

Kenneth raised the iPad again and spoke. "Okay, enough with this disruption. I have the hallowed iPad, so let me speak. We'll hold a special secret ballot and see what the people really want here." He turned his head and glared bug-eyed at Rose for a couple of seconds as she stood smugly with her arms crossed over her chest.

"Dorothy, would you get some index cards and some pens and pass them out so people can cast their votes for the unjustified impeachment of the mayor of Pigeon Ridge?"

Dorothy nodded and exited into the office.

"I want that statement retracted from the record, Kenneth. It's subjective, editorial, and uncalled for," Rose said.

"Well, if we kept a record, perhaps I would, Rose, but as you know, our call for a secretary a while back received exactly zero volunteers. Pedro was the only one with half an interest, and he's not even here anymore, as you well know. So shut up!"

"Damn you, Pedro!" Francine shouted.

Dorothy passed a stack of cards and pens to Arnie, who took one and passed the rest around the room. When they were all distributed, Dorothy spoke.

"Remember, everyone, you are voting to show your support for either Kenneth or Jack as mayor of Pigeon Ridge based on the accusations put forth by Rose. Write-ins will also be accepted."

The residents spent the next few minutes scratching out their votes on the cards. A minute into it, Stanley Foster asked for a new card because he'd messed his up.

"How can you possibly mess up a vote between two people?" Charlene asked in disbelief.

"I don't think that's any of your business, Charlene, so pipe down!" Stanley said.

The two of them glared at each other. It seemed tensions were high between more than just Rose and Kenneth.

When everyone was done, Dorothy gathered up the cards and began tallying the votes. She read each card and kept track of who was winning. When she finished, she said, "The vote totals have been counted. There are fourteen votes for Jack, seven for Kenneth, and one write-in for Sonny Bono. Very funny, whoever you are."

Kenneth's face turned beet red with anger. He raised the hallowed iPad over his head and smashed it on the table in front of him. "This is outrageous! This election was rigged, and it's all your fault, Rose!"

Kenneth stood up and walked over to where Rose was standing. They stood inches apart. Rose spoke first. "What are you going to do, hit a woman, ya loser?"

Provoked by her words, he chest-bumped her and sent her spilling backward onto the floor. He bent down and straddled her, gently restraining her arms with his knees. He started chest-tapping her breastbone with the knuckle of his middle finger. It was a stunt he'd learned while horseplaying with his brothers as the oldest of four boys. The tactic was harmless but annoying as hell, especially when done for extended periods.

As he tap-tap-tapped, he said, "I've never liked you, Rosie. You're always throwing your weight around like you're the queen around here. I've been meaning to put you in your place since I got to the Ridge."

Rose squirmed and struggled, shouting, "Get off me, you boor!"

Objections emanated from the room. "Hey, get off her! We're all adults here."

Suddenly, Big Ed, the sleepy security guard, stood up and approached Charlene's wheelchair.

"Hey, you! Who do you think you are calling me out during the meeting about letting Pedro escape? You made me look like a doofus! I'll show you who's a doofus!"

He grabbed the wheelchair handles, backed her out of the semi-circle, and started pushing her on a slow run down the main hallway toward the cafeteria. His path zigged and zagged, striking fear in poor Charlene, who could only scream defenselessly. Big Ed made zooming and skidding noises with each sharp turn. He wheeled her erratically down to the cafeteria, then made a 180-degree turn and headed back, zigzagging toward the meeting area.

When they reached the room, they saw Arnie standing nose to nose with Laura and poking her in the shoulder with his index finger. "I know it was you who stole my scissors! I saw you lurking around my door the other day after lunch. Now give it back, I said!"

"I don't know what you're talking about, Roger!" Laura said.

"It's not Roger. It's Arnie! Get it right!"

"Well, whoever you are, I did not take your scissors."

The room was an echo chamber of noise and chaos. Two male residents were rolling on the floor, swinging away while accusing each other of stealing the granola bars. Shirley sat in her wheelchair screaming, "Death, take me now!"

Frightened by the chaos, Maureen wheeled over and pulled the fire alarm, and its horn and beacon began beeping and flashing in periodic bursts, adding to the confusion.

Amid the mayhem, an oversized truck pulled up in the horseshoe drive of Pigeon Ridge near the front door. The driver and passenger were dressed in white hazmat suits. They got out and opened the back door of the van. Several others, also in hazmat suits, jumped down from the rear of the truck and stepped into the driveway.

Shirley was the first to speak up. She pointed to the window and shouted, "The aliens are here to get us. Death, take me now!"

"Those aren't aliens, you idiot. They're people in hazmat suits," Big Ed shouted.

All at once, the room quieted down. Kenneth stopped chest tapping, Arnie quit his finger poking, and Stan brought Charlene's wheelchair to a stop near the window. For a few moments, all that could be heard was the beeping of the fire alarm. The rest of the residents all turned and gawked at the white-suited men in the driveway.

Dorothy grabbed the key to the main entrance and let the strangers in. Five of them lumbered in, following behind their obvious leader. He spoke through an amplified megaphone so everyone could hear. Everyone except Lou, of course, who tried to lipread despite the large hood and clear shield covering the head of the speaker.

"Attention, residents of Pigeon Ridge. We are here because your fellow resident, Pedro, was apprehended and arrested for trying to steal Hostess cupcakes and a carton of chocolate milk from a local Kwik Trip station. He disclosed he'd come from Pigeon Ridge after breaking out last night. He said there was dissension building among the leadership around here and things might get violent. From what we can see, that certainly seems to be the case."

"Oh no, there's nothing to see here, gentlemen. I'm in charge here, and we're weathering the sickness quite well, actually. You're free to go," Kenneth said from the floor as he continued to restrain Rose.

The man in the hazmat suit laughed, turned to his assistants, and said, "Did you hear that, fellas? The Lord of the Flies here says there's nothing to see, and we're free to go."

The other hazmat employees in the lobby doubled over in laughter inside their sterile suits.

Francine shouted, "Damn you, Lord of the Flies!"

All That It Seems

Vickie struggled with the latest story she had in her mind. She always loved to write and had started but never finished three different novels. She was good at sketching out a story, but they repeatedly stalled in the middle, and she had a habit of abandoning them in favor of a new idea or, worse, a break from writing altogether. Vickie wasn't sure if it was a fear of failure that kept her from finishing a novel that might meet with a less-than-favorable response or just outright distraction.

On Facebook, she'd seen a reference to ChatGPT, an AI software that could do amazing things. Curiosity got the best of her, so she logged onto the site and created an account. She described the current chapter she was working on and told ChatGPT to create a two thousand word equivalent. Magically, the program typed an entire chapter while she watched. Much of it was flat and nondescript, but when it finished, Vickie sat back in amazement. Her computer had taken a few key sentences and keywords from a human and created a story entirely on its own.

The program made Vickie think of her three unfinished novels. Of the three of them, *Truth Be Told* was the closest to being done. It was the story of a man living in Eau Claire who was secretly married to two different women and maintained a double life. It stalled in the middle when one wife suspected something was going on. Vickie had given up on it three years ago, expecting she'd pick it up at a later date, and the three years had passed quickly.

Vickie sipped her licorice chai tea and then typed into the ChatGPT window:

write 1000 words about Richard's wife getting suspicious of his possible polygamy.

The cursor sprang to life, and words started appearing faster than Vickie could read them. It wrote of Richard's wife finding suspicious clues about her husband and gave Vickie a new set of ideas to work with. Vickie scraped the words from the screen using her mouse and pasted them into a new document. She wasn't sure about the legal implications of using ChatGPT text in a personal manuscript, nor was she sure she would even use them. But she acknowledged it was nice to have the computer take away the need to think for herself. Perhaps she could finally finish her first book after all.

Forbes stood in front of his development team, pointing to the screen projecting his process diagram. The room was dimly lit, and the four software developers watched in various states of attentiveness.

Forbes said, "Again, the advantage of the embedded onboard AI interface on the console of the Huron 9000 autonomous vehicle is its advanced, continual learning. As the car moves, it is in real-time learning mode. If it detects glass or nails twenty yards ahead, it adjusts the travel path of the car to avoid them. Or if the passenger says, 'I don't like how close you're following other vehicles,' the system automatically backs off. Frankly, it's game-changing and will make our car different from those of our competitors."

Shaun spoke up. "Playing devil's advocate here, but how does the AI differentiate good commands from potentially disastrous commands?"

"I'm not sure I'm tracking with you, Shaun. Can you give me an example?"

"Sure. Say you tell the system to drive cautiously because of the snow building up on the roads, and the car interprets that to mean don't drive over thirty miles per hour on the freeway. The car responds by slowing to thirty, and suddenly your vehicle is a menace on the road. I guess what I'm saying is, I don't think you can teach AI common sense."

The room lights up with laughter at Shaun's snarky comment.

"Well, thanks for that insight, Shaun, but in all seriousness, I'd lean toward the thinking that while it may not seem like AI could be trained to have common sense, I think over time it will actually exceed the human capacity for it. After all, the human brain can be aware something is harmful and yet still propel a person to do it anyway. A machine, on the other hand, will be trained in what is wrong one time and never repeat it. The learned behavior is now in the code as a zero, not a one."

Forbes stood there smugly, wearing his certainty, cloaked in confidence.

Shaun raised his pen.

Forbes acknowledged him again. "Shaun?"

"While I get what you're saying about the machine not making the wrong decision twice, I'm just skeptical you can train it for every situation that comes before a driver. At least as humans, we can assess a situation and make an educated guess based on our experience. And it's just my opinion, but I have to think our brains would make a better decision than some machine with a limited storage capacity. Call me old school."

Again, light laughter tittered around the meeting room.

"Well, Old School, I guess you haven't been around the AI code and all of its potential quite as much as me, so you're just going to have to trust me. In fact, I might argue that if anyone here doesn't see the potential and the positives behind the technology, they're welcome to drop off the team. On the other hand, if you want to be part of the next generation of Autonomous Intelligent Vehicles, stick around because, frankly, the sky's the limit."

Sumeesh stared blankly at the screen of his laptop. The mug near him on the small kitchen table of his studio apartment in Madison held an inch of cold coffee. He wasn't sure he liked the direction his life was taking. His communications degree had yet to break him into full-time gainful employment, and his job as a line cook downtown paid the rent but was unfulfilling.

He'd had some small successes with his Patreon account. His quirky videos featuring a blend of magic and humor had gained him a small following of paying viewers, but nothing of financial significance. What he needed was a breakout video like his friend Mari had made. She was a gifted graphic artist whose knack for mixing caustic humor with the macabre made her the success she was. Mari had over eleven thousand followers and was making quite a name for herself.

Sumeesh had long heard about the coming of AI technology and machine learning but wasn't quite sure what role it would play in the lives of ordinary people, let alone an underemployed line cook with an interest in video art. After he'd seen a deep-fake video of Prince playing tennis against Stevie Nicks, he thought there might be some potential to use AI technology to make a video that could earn some good money.

After a little searching on Google, he stumbled upon a product called Vidsmashup. The description made it out to be capable of creating lifelike videos of any person, dead or alive. After you fed it faces, physical feature dimensions, and a scenario, the program went about making up to a three-minute video using the characters and the stated circumstances. It looked like a small startup company with a single developer.

Sumeesh wanted to see for himself what the product's result looked like. He clicked on one of the three video samples on the site. The two-minute video showed a middle-aged Richard Nixon water skiing on a lake. The video was strikingly detailed, including Nixon's pasty white legs. Tricky Dick leaned into a few big turns, spraying large rooster tails as he cut through the glassy water. Sumeesh stopped the video in a couple of places because it looked so real. From Nixon's trademark slicked-back haircut to some tactfully placed liver spots and freckles on his arms, right down to the vintage boat from the seventies.

Sumeesh saw enough to know he wanted to buy the software to give him an edge in his work. He created an account and put in his credit card number.

Vickie looked at her laptop screen with anticipation. The email in her inbox was from her New York agent, Missy Thompson. The subject line read Manuscript Developments. Vickie clicked it open and read:

Hi Vickie,

I have some good news for you. The people at Perfection House love your book! They want to talk to you about a couple of small tweaks, but they are thrilled with the overall story. They want to get going as quickly as possible, so I've attached a contract for your review and signing if you want to go ahead. This is a big New York house, so it is huge for both you and me! Please let me know if you have questions. Otherwise, congratulations, and get back to me ASAP.

Kind regards,
Missy

Vickie sat back in her chair, giddy with excitement. Perfection House! Not too bad! No one would ever need to know that the last third of the book had been largely generated using AI technology. Besides, she'd added her own words in spots, and thus it was more of an embellishment of the actual text ChatGPT had generated. She'd applied her personal flair so she could call it her own. Anyway, how would anyone ever know? It would require them to use the exact keywords she had used to generate the same story. Nope, this one was all hers.

The numbers on the spreadsheet looked dazzling. Forbes read the sales projection attachment from the research and development staff, and he liked what he saw. If they were right, the sales team could move thirty-five thousand cars in the first month of production. The numbers were impressive and attributable to his team's innovation with the AI machine learning interface he'd helped spearhead. People were intrigued by the idea of not only intelligent cars but cars that actually evolved as you drove them. Smart cars getting smarter.

Over time, the AI brain within the vehicle assimilated the drivers' preferences. It could adjust the air temperature, mirrors, seat position, and dozens of other settings, all based on facial recognition. It also corrected the driver's bad habits, like signaling before turns if the driver failed to.

Michael poked his head in Forbes' office door. "Hey, congrats on the Huron thing. That's going to be a sweet payout for you if sales are what they project."

"Thanks. Yeah, I'm pretty psyched. Of course, until I see the profit-share deposit in my account, it's all just talk," Forbes replied.

"Nah, it's a slam dunk. This is a fundamental change in the world of driving, my friend. Kudos. I have a ten o'clock, so gotta run."

"No problem. Thanks for the vote of confidence," Forbes said.

Forbes waved and returned to his work as Michael left.

Sumeesh hit "Watch Again" on the YouTube video he'd made. The video snapped to life. It showed Elon Musk arguing with a homeless woman on a sidewalk. The woman was holding a five-dollar bill Musk had handed her and was visibly angry.

"What the hell do you mean you want change? Do I look like I have change?" the woman said.

"Well then, give it back, you ungrateful loser."

"Here, take it, ya creep! You obviously need it more than I do." The woman crumpled the bill and threw it at Musk, who bent down, picked up the bill, and walked away.

Sumeesh sat back and grinned. He could barely believe the realism he'd created using the Vidsmashup program. Even more unbelievable was the response it had drawn from his followers on Patreon. In the week since it had been released, he'd gathered 4,310 new paying supporters. His PayPal account had blown up, and he was still processing what to do with the more than twenty-five thousand dollars he'd made in the past few weeks. He'd finally found his niche, and all of it was fueled by the Vidsmashup application.

He started brainstorming for his next video. What would it be? Miley Cyrus as an Amish woman milking a goat? Warren Buffet mountain biking in Colorado? Humphrey Bogart rapping, complete with gold chains and a grille?

Vickie abruptly stopped walking and stared transfixed at the screen. She held a cup of black coffee and was on her way home from Ancora Roasters, her favorite Madison coffee shop. She could hardly believe the email she was reading.

Dear Vickie,

It has come to our attention that sizeable portions of your book, "Truth Be Told," were derived from AI technology. After its publication, our plagiarism and authenticity team ran the text through a brand-new AI-sniffing application. Using various AI algorithms and keywords, the application found instances on the ChatGPT site where numerous sections of the book were successfully replicated, word-for-word identical to your novel.

Once this was discovered, the application could target the searches and commands sent to ChatGPT servers from your computer's IP address. These searches were verified as being tied to your username and password, complete with sign-in dates and times. This process has become a new standard for ensuring our readers only get books derived from the authors themselves without the use of computerized creative assistance (CCA).

Based on these findings, it is with significant regret that we will cease production of your book and remove existing stock from all retail and online outlets. Considering the success of your novel, we realize this news will come as a bit of a shock. We at Perfection House are consulting with our legal counsel to see if there are sufficient grounds to seek royalty recovery from you, the author, in the amount of $43,879.64. Our legal staff will reach out to you in the coming weeks to discuss repayment or pending litigation.

Unfortunately, we did not have this AI screening capability before the release of your book, but ultimately, the responsibility for the ethical story creation falls squarely on the shoulders of the author. We are sorry for this news, but at Perfection House the integrity of our authors is one of the core tenets of the house, so we have no choice but to pursue the path of transparency and righteousness.

Sincerely,
The Perfection House Editorial Staff

Vickie's eyes welled up with tears as she stood there, stunned.

"Chatty, take a right at the stoplight," Forbes instructed the beta version interface of the Huron 9000. As chief AI technician, he was also one member of the four-person road test team. The car automatically slowed, engaged the turn signal, and cautiously approached the intersection. The camera sensors were intelligent enough to sense the red light and brought the car to a complete stop, waiting for traffic to clear. Sensing no oncoming impediments, the car slowly accelerated and turned, taking full advantage of the right turn on red—a nuance only an engineer like Forbes could appreciate.

Forbes looked back at his phone. Traveling in an autonomous vehicle made phone surfing entirely safe while driving. Both the driver and any passengers could spend trip time watching TikToks, Instagram Reels, and other mindless social media content while the car did all the work. His latest infatuation was with a guy named Sumeesh. His videos focusing on celebrities were hilarious and incredibly realistic. Forbes liked them so much he'd signed up for Sumeesh's Patreon account.

A Sumeesh reel came on that portrayed Keith Richards dropping into a skate park halfpipe. The soundtrack was "Start Me Up" from the Stones' album, *Tattoo You*. Complete with torn-knee jeans, a red bandana, and his signature hoop earring, Keith rode the pipe up the first rise, then spun in a flawless kick turn. On the return rise, he did a slash turn with ease. He finished out the third rise with a Fakie

Tail Stall, where he came to a full stop, balancing on the board momentarily before dropping back in and flashing the rock-on sign to the camera.

Forbes was transfixed. Everything he saw looked 100 percent legitimate. If that wasn't Keith Richards himself, it was a phenomenal avatar or AI recreation of him. Of course, Forbes knew it was fake, but he marveled at the realism. It made him cognizant that this AI tide was changing the world as he knew it. If some hack named Sumeesh could make something this believable, what were the limits? What could a person believe anymore as actual? What could this potentially do to our governmental system? To the justice system? The possibilities made his head spin. It was a paradigm shifter, for sure.

Forbes looked up momentarily to see where he was. It was mid-morning, and he hadn't had his usual cup of coffee. He thought he'd use the opportunity to evaluate the AI logic.

"Chatty, find me some coffee," he said.

The car engine revved and took a wildly sharp right turn.

Vickie stood there holding her coffee, rereading the accusatory email. By the time she hit the second paragraph, she heard the rev and whine of an engine. The bumper of the car bent her knees backward as she crumpled onto the hood. There was a sickening sound like sticks being snapped, and the thud of her torso as she folded into the front end of the car. Her coffee cup was jarred out of her grasp and hit the windshield, splashing her latte all over the glass. It wasn't until then that the vehicle skidded to a stop.

Forbes sat dazed in the driver's seat and heard the familiar voice of Chatty say, "Your destination is on the windshield."

Divergence

It was a busy afternoon at the Stuckey's restaurant outside Springfield, Illinois. Jennifer wore an apron with a pocket full of tips and hustled between the dining room and kitchen. She was slender with long brown hair and practical jeans, not the bell bottoms that were the fashion of the day for so many teenagers her age. If she ever found the courage to buy them, her parents would probably make her return them to the store, anyway. Hers were proper, church-going parents, and though she was deep into the formation of her own identity, Jen was more the straight-arrow type than a peace, love, rock and roller. She lived firmly in the center lane on the highway of life.

Seated at a table in her co-worker Alison's section were four young hippies. The two women wore their hair long, one pulled back in a ponytail, the other down and held by a fabric headband ringed with small daisies. Both had floral blouses and bell bottoms, ragged and dirty where they dragged on the ground. One of the guys stood out as more mainstream with a traditional haircut, parted to the side, and no facial hair. His buddy was a full-on dude, with a shaggy beard and hair just above his shoulder. Judging from their apparent ideology and lifestyle, neither were the kind of guy Jen would bring home to her parents. She did, however, see the clean-shaven one looking her way every time she passed. Once she even caught his eye, blushing as she did. Nevertheless, she had her standards and felt herself capable of better. The hippie lifestyle just wasn't her groove. Still, it was nice to be noticed.

Alison seemed to wait on them without judgment. She was a much freer spirit than Jennifer, frequently telling Jen jaw-dropping stories of wild weekends with her friends at college. She and the hippies traded laughs in between her trips to and from where they were seated. The table drew stares and gawks from the rest of the patrons. Stuckey's was a family restaurant, and people of this "free love" generation certainly stood out from the pressed shirt and proper haircut crowd.

After more meal hustling, Jen noticed the group had finished their lunch and were paying their bill at the front register. She saw Alison taking off her apron and wondered why. The shift didn't end for another two hours, and she knew Alison was on the same schedule as her. She approached her, "Hey, what's up, Ali? We're on till four."

"I'd love to stay, but these guys invited me to go to Woodstock with them. They have wheels, and it sounds like a fun trip, so I'm going for it!"

"You're what? You can't just leave work, let alone jump town, without telling your parents. That's crazy!"

"I'm going to stop at home, get my money, and pack a bag. I'll leave them a note. They won't like it, but hey, I'm nineteen. What are they gonna do? I figure this is my big chance to see Santana and some of my other favorite bands and live a little, if you know what I'm saying. I've gotta do this, girl. It may be a chance I'll never get again."

"Wow, okay. Well, that's not cool for me because I'll have to pick up your tables, but I guess if you gotta be all peace, love, and groovy, then at least be safe."

"I will. I'll send ya a postcard. Ha!"

The bearded hippie approached Alison and said, "Hey, are you coming?"

"Yeah, I was just telling Jen I'm going to Woodstock."

The hippie added, "Hey, do you want to come too, Jen? It's gonna be far out, sister."

Jen struggled momentarily with his offer. She'd lived her whole life by the book, neatly within the margins, so the thought of doing something as wild as picking up and going to New York State unannounced scintillated in her mind for just a moment. Part of her wished she could be a wild chick like Alison once, just to see what it was like. "Sorry, I've gotta work, and my parents would flip if I did. Thanks for the offer, though."

"Are you sure? We got lots of food and some killer weed. There's room in the car, too."

She'd hoped there wouldn't be any pressure beyond the initial offer. She was already conflicted about not going. This second ask only made things worse. Would she live to regret this decision? Everyone she knew was talking about the big festival and how it was billed as three days of peace and music. At the same time, the idea of dropping everything and hitting the road with her friend and four strangers seemed so far from rational thinking that she couldn't imagine why she'd ever given it a thought. It was a struggle between the allure of the unknown and the security of life as it had always been–safe and antiseptic.

"Yeah, I'm sure. Thank you for the offer, though. I'm not much of a rock music girl."

"Alright, then. We've gotta get truckin'. Don't worry, we'll take care of Alison."

"You better! She's a good friend."

Alison walked over and hugged Jen. "It'll be cool. Don't worry about me. If my parents ask, tell them I'll be home as soon as possible after the festival."

Jen picked up a tray of dirty dishes from a side stand and said, "If you get a chance, write or call me. I'll pay the long-distance charges. Right now, I've got customers waiting for me. Take care, you."

"I will," Ali answered and sauntered out the door with the four strangers.

Jen made her way back to the kitchen. On her way, a customer with his wife and three children stopped her and said, "Miss, we've been waiting twenty minutes for our food. Could you please check on it for us?"

"I'm sorry, sir. Yes, I'll get right on it." She walked away, tray in hand, thinking, *woulda, coulda, shoulda*.

Alison walked along the highway with her new friends. It felt good to be out of the car after hours of driving. The roadway and its ditches were lined with cars, and the entire expressway was closed in the traffic jam to end all traffic jams. It felt like they'd been walking for hours, but at least the weather was good. She'd been drunk plenty of times, but the high she was experiencing after a couple of hits from Dougie's pipe had gone right to her brain. Everything was dreamy.

As she shuffled along, Alison was intently focused on the headband of flowers on the girl in front of her. It was a strange sensation. Ali couldn't explain why this headband seemed so immediately relevant, so demanding of her attention at the moment. Perhaps it was just that she'd never made the connection between how the beauty of nature could bring forth the beauty of humanity. That something fashioned after a flower grown in the earth could set apart the hair of this girl, this stranger, and make her humanity more beautiful. The two elements, flowers and human seemed inextricably connected at this moment.

Alison realized by her sudden fixation that she was stoned, but at this moment, everything in the world seemed right. These people pilgrimaging to a common location, the birds overhead, the grass in the ditches, the occasional rock song coming from a parked car, and even the whiffs cigarette smoke all seemed to have a purpose and place. The world of demanding customers and her serving duties seemed distant. She thought of her friend Jennifer back in Illinois, working away, and wished she could be here to share in the experience. Alison felt so unburdened, like her whole life held something significant to look forward to, and this journey was a step toward it.

Jennifer sat in her bedroom paging through the course guide for the University of Illinois. The fall semester of her third year was imminent, and she wanted to map out her courses. She was pursuing a degree in accounting and business, in part because she was told it was the ticket to a lifelong career. Jen liked the promise of stability, a steady income, and an upward career path after she graduated.

Her mom poked her head in and said, "Hey, I'm sorry to bother you, but Alison's mother called, and she was wondering if you've heard anything from her since she left for the festival?"

"No, I haven't heard a word. She's been on my mind, but Mom, she's a big girl and can take care of herself."

"Yes, I realize she's a wild spirit, but I also understand her mother's concern. She called her mom long distance once a couple of days ago outside Cleveland, but only to check in. She's been part of our prayer group since she left, and I just hope she makes good choices and stays safe."

"I'm sure she's fine, Mom. I've been praying for her too, and I'm a little jealous of her laissez-faire attitude about leaving on a moment's notice."

"Well, you shouldn't be jealous. It just strikes me as irresponsible and selfish, but that's just me. Hanging out with all those hippies and druggies for three days. Blech. Maybe I'm a little old-fashioned," her mother replied.

"Maybe, just a bit. Well, I've got to run. I forgot I'm meeting Tom for lunch at 12:30."

"Okay, hun. Please hug him for me; he's such a dear."
"I will, Mom."

Jen got up and headed to the bathroom to check her hair. As she primped, her thoughts again turned to her friend Alison. It was Saturday, and the concert was likely in full roar. Jen wasn't sure she could fathom being among thousands of rock fans, let alone hundreds of thousands. Her life outside the hippie movement would fully qualify her as a square. At the same time, she couldn't be someone she was not. She was true to herself. She'd been raised in the church with its clear boundaries and strict moral code, and it was all she knew. It was part of her fabric, and she intended to honor it. But, still, she couldn't completely shake the niggling envy of Alison's wildly rebellious act.

The rain pattered incessantly on the tarp covering Alison and Mick, a guy she'd met earlier that day during the Joe Cocker performance. Their attraction in one of the food lines was immediate and mutual. Mick had shoulder-length hair and impossibly green eyes. To add to it were his beaded necklace and his ever-so-subtle East Coast accent. He'd hitchhiked down from Rochester, New York, about three hundred miles from the fest.

The two of them had just finished making love under the tarp and lay together with nothing but an unzipped sleeping bag covering their nakedness. Alison had had sex a couple of times before Mick, but when combined with the mushrooms he'd given her, this experience had seemed otherworldly. Her senses were heightened, and she'd felt connected with him at a spiritual level. It was unlike anything she'd ever experienced. "That was amazingly far out," she said.

"It sure was. I felt like I was floating above us there for a bit," he added.

"So, what do you think it all means?" Alison asked.

"All what?"

"Just everything. Vietnam, the establishment, drugs, the rain. Just *everything*, I guess," she said, trailing off with a giggle.

"Wow, getting all philosophical on me, are you?" Mick grinned at her, unsure if she was serious.

"I am! I guess I'm trying to figure out where my place in life is, and I can only know that if I know where all the rest of it is going. Does that make sense?"

"Yup, it does. These are the things I don't think about much when I'm not high, but they are the things that matter, you dig? I mean, what is the cosmic purpose of all these beautiful souls coming together here just to sing and dance for three days? It's beautifully nihilistic. It means everything and nothing. It is completely irresponsible but also essential to each person's life experience, today and in the future. You follow?"

Alison adjusted the sleeping bag to cover her cold toes, then replied, "Uh-huh, I do. I mean, think about it: if either you or I hadn't come to this place, we wouldn't have met and experienced what we just did. It's a sort of holy moment. What does it mean in the grand scheme of things? I don't know, but it means something significant to my story, and that's enough for me."

"Me too, babe. Wow, you are a deep thinker. I like that in a woman."

She nuzzled into the crook of his arm and tried to rest. It had been a long, trippy day, part of a long trippy weekend, and she was exhausted. The two of them drifted to sleep as the rain continued its patter.

Jen held hands with both of her twin girls, Megan and Monica. The two were dressed in tie-dyed shirts, a gift from her wild friend Alison. The four-year-old girls tended to take off running without notice. With the traffic what it was in Evanston, she made it a point to hold on tight. In some ways, she dreaded grocery day with them, but with Tom working fifty-five-hour weeks at Delatron, time alone was scarce. The pull of the girls on her, physically and mentally, was exhausting, but she tried to make the best of it.

Jen sometimes wondered if she had made a mistake by choosing to stay home with the girls rather than resorting to daycare while she tried to forge a career in the business world. Her friends were all building their futures and moving up in their workplaces while she spent her time feeding and dressing the twins, in between stepping on Barbie shoes and doing dishes. Her business degree was aging not-so-gracefully as it sat in the dresser drawer. She'd never found the time or reason to frame it, and nothing seemed less relevant now that she was committed to raising her girls.

When they got home, she sent them out to play on the swings while she put the groceries away. With food in the house for another week, she checked her mailbox. Amidst the usual junk mail, she came upon a letter from an Alison Grant, no one she knew at first glance. She slit the envelope open, eager to have contact with the outside adult world.

September 17, 1984
Dearest Jen,

I bet you thought I'd fallen off the face of the earth. Well, I haven't, but it's been a crazy ride since I last saw you—lots to tell. I forgot how much I've told you since I saw you last, which, I guess, was probably before I took off for Woodstock seventeen years ago. It's weird how fast time flies, but it's all part of this cosmic journey we're on, I guess.

As you probably figured out by the return address, I'm married...again. Mick (the guy I met at Woodstock, the father of my child, Leo) and I didn't work out. We were young, and I moved in with him up in Rochester after the festival because it seemed like we had such a groove. His struggle to find steady work playing bass, along with both of our struggles with addiction, killed anything we had going for us. C'est la vie, I guess. I took Leo and left Mick, still jobless and searching for some dream he couldn't seem to find.

Anyway, that's just the start of my long, strange trip. I'd love to get together sometime and catch up on what's going on in your life. I miss the old days when we'd go hang out at the Junkhouse Tavern and have a few beers. Such simple times, precious times I'd give my kidneys to have back. Anyway, drop me a letter if you want. It would be great to hear from you.

Love,
Alison

P.S. I hope you got the psychedelic shirts for the girls. Mom told me you had twins!

Jen re-read the letter. She could hardly believe it was her old friend. She'd heard Alison had stayed in New York to settle down after Woodstock, but that was it. It was a bold move in Jen's eyes, but she'd always admired Alison's sense of adventure and carefree attitude. She wished she had half the bravery Alison did. At the same time, she couldn't complain about her own life. The two girls outside swinging were solid proof of all she had to be thankful for.

Later that month, Alison heard a knock at the door. When she opened it, an officer stood holding a paper.

"Good morning, I'm Officer Norwood with the police department. I'm here to serve you an eviction notice. The details are all outlined in this document." He handed the notice to Alison, who quickly scanned the content.

"Hey, wait. It says I only have twenty-four hours to get out. You can't throw me out on the street with only a day's notice! Where am I supposed to go? Can't you cut a person some slack?" Alison said urgently. She was livid at the heartlessness that the cop exhibited while serving her an eviction notice.

"Sorry, miss, but the landlord said you're two months behind on rent." The heavy-set cop with the walrus mustache looked over her shoulder, then continued. "Furthermore, it looks like your living conditions are less than conducive to raising a teenager."

"Don't you tell me how to live! I have my rights!"

"Well, if you're not out by tomorrow afternoon, movers will come to put your belongings on the curb, and those movers will be escorted by yours truly. If you and your son are still here, you will be arrested, and your son will be placed in protective custody. It's your choice. I'm just here to serve notice."

She stood there stewing at his proclamation for a few seconds. "Fine! Go to hell!" Alison slammed the door on the cop, stomped away, and sat in her recliner. She lit a cigarette and looked around. Beer bottles and pizza boxes littered the surfaces of the coffee and end tables. *Living conditions, my ass! I'm a good person. I'm just going through some stuff at the moment.*

She went to her closet and rummaged until she found her suitcase. Cracking it open, she began throwing clothes into it. A few pairs each of jeans, panties, and socks, along with a few blouses and bras. When she was done, she told her son to pack his things. They had nowhere to go, but they couldn't stay here. She had enough going on in her life. She didn't need a police record to go with it.

She lugged her minimal belongings outside, opened the trunk of her twelve-year-old car, and threw in their suitcases. "Okay, Leo, looks like we're camping out in the old Chrysler for a bit until I figure out a plan on where to go."

"Mom, you mean we're sleeping in here? How long do we have to do this?"

"I don't know. Just get in and get comfortable. It'll be our little adventure." Alison lit a cigarette, turned the ignition to accessory mode, and switched on the radio. Jefferson Starship's hit song, "Jane," came belting out of the stereo. *Jefferson Starship, my butt! It's Jefferson Airplane, and without Grace Slick, it ain't worth the vinyl it's pressed on.* Alison had been at Woodstock when Jefferson Airplane—the real deal—sang "White Rabbit" and "Someone to Love." Alison had a mind-blowing experience during White Rabbit, in part because of the hit of LSD she'd gotten from Dougie. One thing was sure; it was a time and a feeling she could never replicate, certainly not from the interior of a Chrysler listening to a bastardization of the band she'd heard over twenty years earlier.

"Jane, Jane, Jane. Pfft!"

She switched off the radio and started the car. She put it into gear and headed into a future full of uncertainty.

It was a cold, drizzly March morning in 1998 as Jen sat in the uncomfortable chair next to her mother's bed in the cancer wing of the hospital. Mom had dozed off, and Jen was momentarily transfixed by the chemo dripping from the bag into the IV and, ultimately, into the veins of her mother. Each drop seemed to represent a moment draining from the bag of her mother's life. Diagnosed with stage four lung cancer, this treatment was a desperate attempt against wild odds to stop or slow the cancer. Her mom had agreed only because Jen was so adamant she try it. It was a crapshoot but was all they had to go on.

Jen heard a slight tap, tap on the open door. She turned to see her friend Alison standing there. At least, she thought it was. She hadn't seen her since she left for Woodstock so long ago. If it was her, she'd gained some wrinkles and a few gray hairs but had managed to maintain her figure over the years, unlike Jen, who'd never entirely lost her post-pregnancy weight.

"Alison?" she said. Alison just nodded her head and covered her mouth and quietly broke out in tears. Jen rose from the chair and walked over to her friend, whom she hadn't seen for over two decades. The two fell into each other's arms in a long, emotional hug Jen had waited for since she saw Alison walk out of Stuckey's that August day in 1969.

Through her sobs, Jen said, "It is so good to see you. I wondered where you'd been and what was going on in your life."

"Oh, girl, my life is a story to tell. But more importantly, I'm here for you. Mom told me about your mother's cancer. How is she doing?"

"Not good, but we're in round two of chemo, so trying to stay positive, you know?"

"Yeah. I do. I'm so sorry this is happening," Alison replied.

"Well, if there's one thing I've learned since you walked out of work that day, it's that nothing in life is static or permanent. Except good friends."

"Ain't that the truth?"

"Hey, Mom just drifted off. Do you want to go down to the cafeteria and talk? We've got a lot to catch up on," Jen asked.

"Sure, I could use a cup of coffee."

They followed the blue line on the hospital floor, which led to the elevators. The elevator took them to the first floor, where the cafeteria was located. They paid for their drinks and found a table.

"So, for starters, tell me all about Woodstock," Jen said.

"Oh, so long ago, Jen. It was weird, wild, and wonderful, with a dash of miserable all at the same time. I mean, the message and music were amazing. People were full of love, and everyone was so cool. It was a great vibe, albeit in the rain and mud, for much of it. I'm glad I went and, well, I wouldn't have my Leo if I hadn't. Of course, I wouldn't have my past with that loser Mick either. Somewhere in the haze of my life at that time, I battled addiction and the bottle, too. I even lived in my car for a month. But I've straightened out and cleaned up for the most part."

"Wow. Quite a story. A strange question, but which performance did you like best? Over the years, I've become obsessed with having missed a chance to go to such a landmark event."

Alison reared her head back, laughed, and put her hand on Jen's. "Oh, that's easy. Santana! All the groups were good, but I loved Santana. They were fantastic! It's been a wild ride since then, probably wildly different than your journey."

Jen took a sip of her coffee and began. "Well, compared to yours, mine is all white bread and milquetoast. Boring as hell, relatively speaking. I got my degree in business and married my college crush, Tom. We had twin girls, Monica and Megan. Tom has worked at Delatron for the last eighteen years, while I stayed at home with the girls. Now I'm working part time as an administrative assistant at a school here in town. A dog, a cat, a white picket fence in the burbs, the whole nine yards. Boring!"

"Actually, I am a little jealous. You've done things the way I should have all along."

"Well, at the same time, I'd give anything to have had the experiences you've had. Woodstock, moving from your home state, starting over, heck, even living in a car for a bit. Your story just seems so much more interesting than mine."

Alison ran her fingers through her hair, looked her friend in the eye, and said, "Well, as I have grown older, I've realized there's no one to stop us from taking wrong turns or traveling down dead-end roads. We're all speeding toward something that we construct in our minds, and every outcome is different. For you, happiness took the safe route–and it worked for you. For me, happiness took some pain, upheaval, and corrections along the way. Ultimately, we have to go with our gut. Leave Stuckey's. Stay at Stuckey's. Both answers are right, and both are wrong. You see what I mean?"

"You know, I never thought of it that way. By reconnecting and sharing our stories, I've sort of relived the life I could have had through yours, and you through mine. Like human books!" Jen replied.

"Exactly. Parallel but divergent lives. Neither is right or wrong. Both are beautiful and unique."

"I love that. Here I've been beating myself up for years thinking I missed out on something, only to find out you've been doing the same thing?" Jen asked.

"Yep. Bingo."

The two of them broke into quiet laughter at their revelation. They finished their drinks and made their way back to the cancer ward.

It was a warm August afternoon in 2019 as Jen maneuvered her way through suburban Chicago traffic toward the Hollywood Casino Amphitheater. Alison sat in the passenger seat gazing through sunglasses at the wispy clouds over the glass, concrete and steel of strip malls.

"Hey, Jen, since this is a concert and all, want to have some fun?"

She turned to see Alison pulling something out of her purse. "What is that?"

"It's a medicinal Cannabis chocolate bar. I take it as a prescription for situational anxiety. I'm not going to lie that I also take a piece for recreational purposes, on occasion," she said with a laugh. "It'll get you feeling really good in about an hour. Sorta like getting high without the smoke," Alison explained.

"I thought you cleaned up?"

"Like I said, I did…mostly. This medicinal cannabis is legal in lots of places now. It's harmless, and besides, it's a miracle cure for my anxiety."

"Well, I've never done anything like this, but, hey, at my age, why not?"

"You know, you only live once," Alison said, handing her the chocolate square.

"It'll take a bit to kick in, but we will be in our seats by then. It should wear off by the time the concert is over."

"Cool. Who would have thought we'd be here together, fifty years after Woodstock, almost to the day, going to see Santana, with me getting high for the first time in my life at seventy-two?"

"At an outdoor venue, nonetheless. This is our little Woodstock of the Midwest! Peace, sister!"

Alison flashed the peace sign, and Jen smiled and flashed one back. As she did, she thought how lucky she was to be here with her longtime friend. Their lives had run courses as different as anyone could have imagined. And when it came right down to it, neither was right nor wrong. Simply different. Their divergent lives had ultimately brought them to this moment.

Over time, despite their differences, their friendship held firm. Jen's regret about not going to Woodstock to experience the peace, love, and music was something she couldn't go back and change. But at the moment, she was making up for it by doing all three. It was a cheap suburban substitute for the music festival that changed a generation, but it was all she had. It was also exactly what she needed.

As she turned the corner toward the parking area, Jefferson Airplane's "Somebody to Love" came on the radio. When Grace Slick's signature voice belted out the opening lyrics about the truth being found to be lies, Alison reached over and turned up the volume.

"This is a great song!" Alison said.

Jen was reminded that long ago she had found somebody to love.

Children of Mother Earth

Tilted Thomas walked with quite a lean. His left shoulder dropped, and his right jutted skyward as if held by a sadistic puppeteer. Everything on his body was proportional, but when he stood "straight," his spine angled like the hour hand of a clock set to 1:30, and his hips were wildly out of level and off-kilter. In fact, his entire body was tilted.

When his parents first saw the condition in Thomas' posture and spinal alignment, they figured it was some sort of birth defect or unfortunate genetic disorder. They spent thousands of dollars sending Thomas to doctors and specialists, only to be told, "There's nothing wrong with your son. He's perfectly normal and, unless he's in apparent pain or uncomfortable, there's nothing we recommend."

When Thomas was four years old, Dr. Lewis measured his spinal tilt and found it to be exactly 23.5 degrees. Because Dr. Lewis was also an astronomy geek, he quickly made the connection. He knew immediately that the tilt angle matched that of the Earth relative to its axis. He was so excited at his findings that he started the process with the American Medical Association (AMA) of getting the affliction named after himself; Lewisian Terrestrial Tiltitus. Until the AMA could research and adopt it as an official medical condition, Thomas was just referred to as being terrestrially adjusted.

Once a definitive diagnosis was made, his parents gave up trying to fix Thomas. His condition was his body's one-of-a-kind response to an offset no one else on the planet felt.

As he grew, Thomas struggled in school because of the incessant teasing and occasional bullying. Kids called him Tilted Thomas and walked by him in the hallways, leaning the opposite way, mocking his unnatural bentness. This teasing bothered Thomas. It wore on him. He hated his situation. He hated himself and his disorder.

The school administration was very cognizant and responsive to his unique situation providing him with a specially designed desk to accommodate his 23.5-degree lean. Without it, his writing always started in the upper left of the page but quickly dropped off the bottom as the pull of gravity was simply too much to endure as he wrote. After his new desk was built, his writing was straight, clean and normal. The school also had a plumbing contractor come in and construct a custom-slanted private toilet in the boys' restroom. No easy feat!

One day after kindergarten, Thomas asked his mother, "Mom, am I different from other kids?"

"Now, Thomas, why would you ask such a thing?"

"Mason at school said I wasn't like all the other kids. He called me a gimp."

His mother was quick to address his insecurity. "Oh, Thomas, that's a mean thing to say. Doesn't Mason know all people are different? Some are short, some tall, some black, others white, some tilted, some straight."

Thomas looked at his mother. "That's what I thought, Mom. Mason's kind of mean to a lot of kids."

Tilted Thomas' parents tried to make a normal life for him. They had a special bike made by Adaptive Athletics, a company specializing in designing equipment for people with disabilities. The head engineer gave his father a quizzical look when he explained he wanted a bike built at a 23.5-degree angle.

"So, the tires would be round, just squeejawed to one side, then?"

"Squeejawed?" Thomas' father asked.

"Oh, sorry. Yeah, squeejawed is what I call anything that is tilted, or off-square," the engineer clarified.

"Huh, that's a great word. But yes, build a bike, just make it squeejawed by 23.5 degrees."

Five hundred and eighty-seven dollars later, Tilted Thomas rode his tilted bike in synchronicity with the squeejawed planet Earth. As he perilously leaned his way down the block, speeding on his custom cruiser, people often honked their horns in amazement. He looked like an impending disaster averted only by the speed of his forward thrust; a constant left turn somehow moving straight as an arrow. Thomas loved his bike. He felt confident on it, like he could do anything behind the handlebars of his tilted two-wheeler.

Shortly after his eighteenth birthday, a circus representative came to their door and asked his mother if she thought her son would like a career riding his angled bike in their high-wire act. A neighbor had seen him riding around the neighborhood and tipped off Borkem and Bilkem's Circus about Thomas' unique abilities. The representative assured her it would be a one-of-a-kind act, nothing else like it in the world. "It would be an opportunity for fame no one should pass up," the rep said.

Thomas' mother took great offense at the offer. "My son is not a freak! He's terrestrially adjusted. Do you understand? The answer is NO!" she said, slamming the door in the rep's face.

As an adult, Leadfoot Lisa got her nickname from her shoes. Most people assumed it was related to her driving habits when, in fact, driving was quite impossible since her shoes were primarily made of lead. If she were ever granted a driver's license, it would, in essence, be a license to kill. The thought of her foot anywhere near a gas pedal, or a brake for that matter, was frightening. With Leadfoot Lisa, it would be pedal-to-the-metal starts followed by body-through-the-windshield stops. When you wear lead shoes, there's no middle ground.

Lisa was born with the world's only known case of Gravitational Deficit Disorder. It was first discovered at birth. When the doctor tried to lay Lisa on her mother's chest, she floated six inches above her. Everyone in the delivery room gasped when they saw her floating there, just blinking at her mom. Her mother, Julia, gently grabbed Lisa, pulled her to her chest, and whispered, "I love you, sweetie." When she let go, Lisa rose back up above her mother again. Julia looked at the doctor with questioning eyes. The doctor's jaw dropped as he raised his eyebrows and shrugged. What they all were witnessing was like a magic trick no one wanted to see.

After months of trips to dozens of specialists who conducted batteries of tests, no doctor could explain the phenomenon. There certainly was no history of levitation in the family and, despite poring over volumes and volumes of medical data, there didn't appear to be any other cases of it worldwide. Lisa was her own living resurrection.

As a baby, her condition was easy enough to deal with. Straps were cinched tight in highchairs, strollers, and car seats, so it was simple enough to disguise. At bedtime, she was laid in her crib with a blanket draped over her and a tall pillow for her head as she hovered nine inches above the mattress. The first time Julia laid her down and pulled the blanket over her, her husband Rufus chuckled a little.

"What are you laughing at?" she asked.

"I can't help but think she looks a little like a David Copperfield levitation act, except smaller."

"Rufus! Really? You stop that right now. She's beautiful."

"Sorry, honey. Yes, she is. She's perfect," he replied.

At eleven months, Lisa was showing signs of walking. Her gravitational deficit made this new stage a bit of a dilemma for Rufus and Julia. Julia brought home a pair of toddlers walking shoes. When she put them on Lisa and stood her up, Lisa couldn't do anything but swing her feet wildly in the air. She looked like a baby Michael Jackson moonwalking across the living room.

"Well, that's not going to work now, is it?" Julia said in a tone of desperation.

Rufus just stood there, perplexed and stupefied. "Maybe we should get her a pair of those shoes that have been bronzed after a baby has grown out of them." Rufus chuckled at his joke.

"Rufus! You be nice." Julia said.

"Sorry, hun. We have to keep our sense of humor about this, though."

"I know, but sometimes, it's all just too much."

"I have some ideas on how to get her grounded and walking, so I'll work on them this week. My daughter's going to have a normal life if it kills me," Rufus said.

That week he set to work making her first pair of lead-soled shoes.

Thomas took the final turn at top speed on his tilted racer. The velodrome crowd roared as he sprinted toward the finish line. Once again, he'd won by a margin of three laps over the second-place racer, setting a new Olympic record and winning the gold medal. The additional 23.5 degrees of lean through the curves propelled him forward with incredible velocity. On the straightaways, he took the inside lane where his lean helped him perch on the edge of the track that other riders could not. This cut several meters off the total distance of travel, helping shave his time even more.

Despite being contested as having an advantage, the International Olympic Committee rejected the claims and declared him a legitimate athlete. He suffered through several invasive physical exams and medical records requests to ensure he hadn't intentionally changed his skeletal structure to his benefit. His parents came to his defense on a couple of occasions, testifying to his condition being present at birth.

Once established as a fully qualified participant in the sport of velodrome racing, his track times were changing the sport forever. After years of working his way up the channels, this was his first Olympics, and he was coming away with a gold medal. Because he was so heavily favored coming into the games, the IOC anticipated his victory by creating a hydraulic-powered center podium slanted at 23.5 degrees in tribute to his triumph over his condition.

Thomas stood crookedly tall with his hand over his heart as they played the National Anthem over the sound system. Tears welled up in his eyes as thoughts of his past struggles and tribulations raced in his head. All the teasing and bullying he suffered in his school years, and all the training he did to get himself to this point, came to mind and overwhelmed him. As he looked at the fake American flag blowing on the video screen, it occurred to him he'd finally done it. He had overcome. He had achieved the pinnacle of his young life at age twenty-four. Only one thing was missing, he thought. Someone to share his life with.

Despite an increasing levitational height as she aged, Leadfoot Lisa tried as much as possible to have a normal life. This included her desire to date. In her early twenties, she browsed the UniquelyMe.com matchmaking site with curiosity and hope. She'd heard about the site from her friend Transparent Theresa, whose inability to control her level of transparency pushed her to start the site for normal people with supranormal disorders. Theresa was tired of being practically invisible to men.

Lisa scrolled past the obvious non-matches. Guys like Lunar Larry, who gained an inch in height every day during the lunar cycle, only to reverse the process and shrink by an inch the same way for the next cycle. Dating someone who was five-foot ten inches at the beginning of the cycle and over eight feet tall at the end just seemed daunting to Lisa. There were other guys like Barnacle Bud, whose skin grew a three-day growth of barnacles whenever it was exposed to water. His profile said he only showered once a week to help minimize the condition. Lisa was big on personal hygiene and soft skin, so Bud was definitely out.

After scrolling for twenty minutes, Lisa took off her leaden shoes and levitated near the ceiling with her phone as she came across the profile for Tilted Thomas. The opening description of his condition struck home with her. The tilt of the earth's axis and its gravity were both unseen planetary phenomena, and at the core of both of their unique makeups. They were Earthmates! One sentence especially piqued her interest.

Looking for a woman who is capable of being both well-grounded but not afraid to reach for the stars and even try to fly every once in a while.

It sure seemed like a perfect match from where she floated. Lisa clicked the "Let's meet!" button and tapped out her greeting.

With the Olympics behind him and not happening again for four years, Thomas wondered what was next. He planned to continue biking as it provided him with a sense of purpose, and he reveled in the thought of setting records that might not be broken for years to come. But there had to be more. He felt a need for romantic personal connections in his world. He revisited the UniquelyMe.com website where he'd set up his profile a couple of weeks prior. The description of the matchmaking site captured his interest. It read:

UniquelyMe.com thinks every person deserves someone to love. Our service focuses on people with special—one might even say gifted—qualities. All applicants are screened for authenticity to ensure that you will only meet other specially gifted singles. UniquelyMe.com - Creating relationships that were meant to be…unique!

Thomas was ecstatic when he'd found the site. It was hard enough dealing with his gifts among people who knew him. Trying to find someone who could relate to his condition seemed almost hopeless. UniquelyMe.com seemed like his best option.

He reviewed his profile and started scrolling through the list of female matches. Sleepless Suzanne was beautiful, and her bio sounded interesting. Her ability to go sleepless for fourteen straight days, only to sleep for fourteen, seemed daunting, however. Thomas was a light sleeper, so the thought of her being up and around while he tried to sleep quickly put that idea to bed.

Frosty Francine was also attractive, but the thought of the room cooling down by fifteen degrees Fahrenheit every time she walked in seemed like a deal breaker. She might be a better match for Hot Blooded Harold, a friend Thomas had met in an online gaming room exclusively for uniquely gifted people.

He scrolled through the multitude of names. Nightvision Nancy, Rubberneck Rebecca, Mindreader Mindy, Timejump Tammy, and Shapeshifter Sharon. None caught his interest. He even ventured over to the physically gifted section of the site just for giggles. The names and pictures there were both beautiful and a little shocking to him. Names like Lobster-claw Laura, Skinless Scarlett, Yeti Yolinda, and Webfoot Wendy all held their attractiveness to him, but none swept Thomas off his slanted feet.

When he was about ready to give up, a notification bubble popped up in his message box. He clicked the message excitedly.

Hi Thomas,

Let's Meet! My name is Leadfoot Lisa, and I read your bio three times thinking we'd be a great match. I'd love to meet you for coffee or dinner or just a short walk somewhere. Obviously, long walks tire me out given my special footwear, but I am working on increasing my leg strength every day, so I can do more of what I want to do, like see the world. It's my goal to one day run a 5K race. Lofty? Yes. (And I know a lot about loft, let me tell you. LOL.) But what is life if you don't set goals? I mean, look at what you've accomplished!

Anyway, I've rambled enough. If you think you'd like to get to know me a little better, inbox me or give me a call. My number is in my profile. Thanks! – Lisa

Thomas could hardly believe what he was reading. No one had ever expressed an interest in him for anything other than his athletic achievements. To have someone reach out with romantic intentions felt oddly unnatural, weird, and wonderful all at the same time. Lisa was attractive, with auburn hair, high cheekbones, and stunning features. The fact that her picture showed her floating near the ceiling of her apartment meant she had a good sense of humor. Her bio showed she had similar interests, including art and science fiction novels. Best of all, she lived only fifteen minutes away, so a meet-up certainly seemed viable.

Thomas replied to her message.

Hi Lisa. I got your note and would love to meet you! Would you like to get together for coffee sometime next week? I'd be happy to arrange something near you. Let me know.

Thanks, Thomas.

He clicked send and smiled to himself at the direction his life seemed to be taking.

Thomas leaned his tilted bike against the No Parking sign and slanted his way into Gravity Coffee, home of the atomic latte. The aroma of coffee and cinnamon rolls washed over him as he entered. All the baristas there knew his name and brew of choice.

"Good afternoon, Thomas!" the barista said.

"Hey Monique, how are you today?"

"I'm good. How about you?"

"Well, I'm meeting a date here, so I am leaning toward fantastic," Thomas replied with a grin.

"Ha, ha! Good one. A date? So that is pretty great. Can I make you an atomic latte?"

"That would be outstanding, thank you."

As he waited for the drink, the front door swung open. In walked Lisa, her steps slow and labored, each one resonating like a brick hitting the floor. He caught her eye as she worked her way toward him like a skier walking in ski boots. Heel, toe, clomp, clomp. Her hair and green eyes caught the light, making Thomas giddy with anticipation and excitement. Her deliberate gait and Frankenstein stride might appear awkward to some, but to Thomas, it had all the sex appeal of a supermodel on a runway.

When she reached him, she leaned to one side and gave him a brief hug. "So good to meet you, Thomas," Lisa said.

"The pleasure is all mine. Can I get you a coffee?"

"Yes, I'll have a cappuccino, thank you," she replied.

When their drinks were ready, they took them to a table near the window. Thomas had his custom-made cup slanted at 23.5 degrees. The coffee house had gone to special lengths to get them made by their packaging distributor to accommodate Thomas' uniqueness. They'd even had a special tilted table installed just for Thomas. Gravity Coffee prided itself on being an ADA-conscious business. Both modifications paid dividends because Thomas was there every day, often twice a day, getting coffee.

Lisa noticed the slant of the cup and said, "Wow, it's amazing that the cup doesn't tip over."

"Yeah, packagers are doing some crazy things with counterbalancing these days."

Throughout the afternoon, Thomas and Lisa discovered they had much in common. Both liked a few of the same bands, both admitted they were art-loving introverts, and both hated politics. Thomas admitted his favorite ride at the fair was the Tilt-a-Whirl, while Lisa said hers was the Rotor, where the floor dropped out while people were flung against the spinning walls, held in place by centrifugal force.

After a one-year courtship, Thomas and Lisa got engaged. Their uniqueness brought them together. Lisa adored Thomas' racing skill and his ability to crack self-deprecating jokes, especially the running joke he'd always thought he'd marry someone named Eileen. Or that his favorite song was "Lean on Me" by Bill Withers. Lisa mentioned hers was "Feeling Gravity's Pull" by R.E.M. Thomas and Lisa were stout advocates for people with "speciabilities," a term they'd coined combining the words special and abilities. It was their way of neutralizing the term disability, which had such a negative connotation and tone to it. They both felt that while their conditions were part of their makeup and what set them apart from others, keeping a sense of humor about it was important too.

After Thomas' Olympic success, he made vast sums of money in endorsements, mainly because of the mega-selling "Tilted Thomas Lean Burger," a hamburger featuring a much leaner mix of meat than ordinary burgers. He was an American hero, complete with an action figure, lunch box, and video game. It carried over into the beverage industry as well, where his Tilted Thomas Terrific Tea, a caffeinated performance-enhancing bottled tea, became a hit both in the states and abroad. His endorsements set him up for life.

The money meant nothing to Lisa. She was hopelessly smitten with her new husband and worked anyway. She got a job at a local warehouse as the supervisor in charge of inventory. Her aptitude for numbers and attention to detail were key attributes for doing the job well. On top of that, when necessary, she could step out of her shoes and slowly float to the ceiling of the multi-story warehouse, enabling her to see inventory out of view of people on the ground. It was a skill she only used on occasion and had not been on her resume. Her employers were happy with the new level of inventory accuracy it provided, despite the probable OSHA violations it presented.

Their life was on a good track when one day Lisa said, "Thomas, are you sitting down?" Thomas answered from his crooked recliner in the other room. "Yes, I am, honey. What's up?"

"I'm pregnant."

"You're what? Oh my goodness, honey, that is fantastic! We're going to have a baby!" He walked over to her and hugged her tightly.

"Yes, we are. Frankly though, as happy as I am, I'm a little worried about the mix of our genetics. I hope everything turns out okay."

"Honey, every person in this world is unique. Between you and me, our combined speciabilities are both one in a multi-million shot. That makes our child closer to one in a billion, and I can't wait to meet him or her."

"I guess I didn't look at it that way, but you're right. We are pretty lucky to have each other, and this child will certainly have its share of love," Lisa replied.

"Exactly. Let's not overthink it, shall we? We're going to have a baby!" he said as he leaned in and gave her another crooked hug.

Leadfoot Lisa strained, pulling hard at the straps on her arms and legs that held her down. It was obvious that during childbirth, she couldn't be floating above the bed. While the child she had in her womb decreased her loft over the past few months, she could still levitate to twenty-five feet without her lead shoes. Her discomfort and pain were etched on her face as she moaned and writhed on the confining delivery bed. There was nothing Thomas could do but hold her hand and feed her ice chips when she asked. The feeling was helpless.

After a seven-hour labor, a beautiful baby girl was brought into the world. From a physical standpoint, there was no evidence she had the spinal slant Thomas was born with. This brought relief to everyone in the room as they waited to see if the baby would levitate like Lisa had at birth. When the doctor laid the baby on Lisa's chest, she squirmed there but remained grounded. Lisa flashed a look at Thomas and then at the doctor.

"Oh, Thomas, look, she's beautiful and perfectly normal."

"Of course I am. What did you expect?" the baby replied.

Lisa and Thomas looked at one another and gasped.

"Oh, my goodness. She can already talk!"

"Bien sur je peux."

Thomas, who had studied French in high school, translated. "She just said, 'Of course I can.'"

"Bueno, ¿me vas a dar un nombre o no?" the baby said.

This time, Dr. Esperanza translated. "She wants to know if you're going to give her a name or not."

Lisa looked at Thomas with wide eyes, unsure what to think. "Well, we were thinking if it was a girl, we'd name her Paula," she said.

"Ich liebe es!" ("I love it," in German) baby Paula said.

And thus, Polyglot Paula was born into the world.

Tea in the Pacific Northwest

The sweat on Michael's forehead dripped into his eyes, stinging with its saltiness as he worked his way up the trail—or at least he thought it was a trail. He wasn't entirely sure he hadn't errantly wandered onto a deer trail of some sort. Something told him he might have taken a wrong turn at the fork a hundred yards earlier. He checked his phone, but there was no reception this deep in the Oregon forest, so he was left to intuition. He decided he'd give it another hundred yards, and if it didn't look more promising, he'd retrace his steps to the fork where he thought he might have made the wrong turn.

Michael lumbered forward, scanning deep into the trees immediately ahead as well as the periphery. A light mist rained down, giving everything a surreal feel and making details that were once clear, fuzzy. Peering into the forest off to his left, he saw a bulge at the base of one of the towering Douglas Firs in the distance. He stopped and lingered for a closer look. The large aberration was covered in green moss and stuck out like a huge wart. The structure looked tall enough to stand in.

Curiosity got the better of him, and he stepped off the trail toward the hut. He picked his way carefully through ground-hugging ferns, over logs and other decay on the forest floor. He worked his way quietly, not wanting to startle whatever lived in this makeshift hut. It was covered in lichens and moss, with much of the exterior constructed of a combination of pine branches and large chunks of tree bark. He walked around the structure looking for an entrance and found one on the eastern side of the tree. Whoever built this thing knew enough to put the door on the sheltered side of the weather.

Michael slowly pulled open the pine-bough door. He peered in to see a gigantic hairy beast holding a book and staring back at him. The beast had a huge forehead and matted, gnarled hair from head to toe. Off to one side of the interior was a fire pit with extinguished residue from past fires. A few wooden dishes were stacked near it, and beside them, a pile of small bones from a rabbit or squirrel sat stripped clean on a layer of fern leaves. The hut smelled of sweat, bad breath, and stale smoke. Michael froze in total fear as he and the beast locked gazes for a few awkward seconds.

"Can I help you?" the beast said in perfect English.

Michael raised his eyebrows in surprise. "Uh, sorry. What? You can speak?"

"Yes, sir. As can you, apparently," the beast replied.

Michael's heart hammered in his chest, ramping up for fight or flight. He had only seconds to decide whether to make a run for it or stay put and see what happened. It seemed, at least in this first verbal exchange, that this Sasquatch, or whatever it was, was friendly.

"Yeah, I can speak. Um, I guess this might sound strange, but can I come in?"

"Surely. There's a log for you over there," it said, gesturing to a nearby makeshift seat. "Make yourself at home."

Michael tried to fathom what was happening. Though it was sitting, the beast had to stand at least seven feet tall, judging from the torso and the size of its limbs. Even stranger, he had just set down a tattered copy of Kurt Vonnegut's classic, *Slaughterhouse Five,* which he'd been reading before Michael's interruption.

"Thank you. You are too kind," Michael responded.

"Is there such a thing as too much kindness?" the beast asked.

"What? I mean, no. I guess not. It's just a saying we have among us humans."

The beast tilted its head as though it didn't understand.

"It's hard to explain," Michael said. "It's a saying we use that means well but probably ends up sounding negative. A sort of nuance of the language, you see."

The beast nodded but did not appear convinced. "Would you like something to eat? I have dried mushrooms or some fresh lichens."

Michael saw a small pile of mushrooms and other foraged items nested in one corner. "No, thank you. Can I offer you some trail mix, though? I'm guessing you've never had anything like this. It's a mixture of chocolate, raisins, nuts, and dried fruit."

The beast furrowed its brow in apparent interest. "Sounds like something I need to try."

Michael pulled a plastic Ziploc bag out of his coat pocket and opened it. He reached across and offered some to the beast who reached out with long, weathered fingers and took some from the bag. It looked at the small pile in its palm, then picked up a shelled peanut between thumb and forefinger, eyeing it suspiciously.

"Never seen a nut like this."

"Those are peanuts. They grow underground. Try it."

The beast popped the nut into its mouth, chewed, and swallowed it. "Mmmm…that's quite good."

"Yeah, they're my favorite nut. But hey, try one of the colored candies. They're called M&M's. The secret is in the center."

Again, the beast picked one from his open palm, eyed it, and popped it in its mouth. After chewing it for a few seconds, it turned its head and spat the remnants of the candy onto the dirt floor. "Ackaka! That tastes like deer dung! Do you humans really eat these things?"

Michael laughed nervously and nodded his head. "Yes. It's called chocolate and is considered a sweet treat among humans."

"Ackaka! Horrible stuff!" The beast set the rest of the trail mix on a makeshift table and reached and dipped a wooden cup into a hollowed-out log with water in it. It took a swig, rinsed its mouth out, and spat.

Michael laughed quietly and apologized. "I'm sorry. I thought you'd like those."

The beast wrinkled its nose and spat again.

"If you don't mind, I have to ask. You're a Bigfoot, right?"

The beast looked down at its hairy feet, then at Michael's feet, then its own again. "I take that personally, sir."

Michael reeled and tried to reframe the question. "No, no, no. I didn't mean that as a personal attack, but Bigfoot is a slang term for what we humans call your kind." The beast again tilted its head as though it didn't understand. Michael slid his boot next to the beast's, showing the obvious difference. "See? Your feet are massive compared to the human foot. But yes, I can see how you might think it offensive."

"Frankly, yes, I do. We don't call humans 'smallfoots.' To us, they're just humans."

Michael collected his thoughts and smiled warmly to reassure the beast he meant no harm. "Actually, to us humans, your species, or your kind, are known as Sasquatch."

"Oocka, oocka, oocka!" The beast slapped its knee and rocked back on its log, overcome with laughter. It chortled and shook for a full ten seconds in apparent amusement. "Sasquatch? That's what you call us? That's no better than Bigfoot. Oocka, oocka!"

This was the second show of playfulness from the beast, and it made Michael's heart sing. Maybe these creatures had been given a bad rap all along. So far, it seemed they were gentler than most humans he'd met. Or at least more polite, not to mention more well-spoken.

Michael glanced at the Vonnegut book sitting on the log next to the beast. "So, you can read?"

"Oh, yes, I love a good book. You don't happen to have any with you, do you?"

"Actually, I do have a Michael Crichton book," he replied. He pulled off his pack, dug down, and got the book. He handed it to the beast, who immediately turned it over and read the back cover.

"Huh. I'm a big Michael Crichton fan, except for Jurassic Park. Everyone knows dinosaurs could never have happened."

Michael grinned at the irony. Here he was talking to a beast that many people thought didn't exist, and here the beast thought the same of dinosaurs. "Well, actually, they've discovered many dinosaur fossils from millions of years ago. Some would even say Sasquatches are descendants of cave dwellers who lived during the age of the dinosaurs. In fact, one of the oldest human skeletons found was over 3.6 million years old. Ironically enough, they named it Little Foot," Michael said with a grin.

The beast tilted its head to the side in an apparent attempt to understand. "Oocka, oocka, oocka!" the beast laughed. "You humans are obsessed with foot size."

"I never thought of it that way, but yes, it appears we are. So, back to the book. How did you learn to read, let alone get ahold of books?" Michael asked.

"Well, the English vocabulary of my parents was passed on to me. From there, I took it upon myself to read as much as I could, which increased my literacy and grammar significantly. The English language is pretty simple, especially for creatures like me, considering the size of my brain. I don't mean to brag here, but your language is nothing special. For years, our colony has communicated using a complex language of more than 50,000 grunts, clicks, and hand gestures. Since English was assimilated, it has dumbed down our culture."

Michael laughed at the comment, and his eyes drew again to the size of the beast's head. It was much larger than an ordinary human head. Even weirder was the sagittal crest running from the top of its forehead to the back of the skull. Was there more brain matter tucked into this narrow ridge? If so, it would help explain a lot about the intelligence the beast was displaying.

Michael shifted on his log and crossed his leg at the knee. His interest in this beast was keen. His simple hike in the forest was quickly turning into an anthropological interview of an unknown culture and people group. Early in his undergraduate years at the University of Minnesota, he'd taken a fair number of anthropology classes and was cognizant of the need to understand, yet not impact, the people being studied.

"So, you said you read as much as you can. Where do you get your books?"

"From the town landfill. You humans throw away a lot of stuff! But I go in search of books and magazines only. I've got a few novels on hand; the rest I've loaned out to friends and family. Believe me, though, it's tricky getting them at night. To go in broad daylight would be suicide for me. I've read enough novels about your guns and your thirst to kill."

The comment drew a sober look from Michael. Here was a beast previously assumed to be primitive and simple-minded, calling out the human race for its inhumanity to one another. The beast had a point, and in a way, it made Michael ashamed to be part of all of it.

"Tell me, how far back does your history go? How long have you been in this area of North America?"

"While I am sure it goes back thousands of years, we Malterns are not gifted with good long-term memories and thus don't have an oral history to draw from. At best, we can remember back ninety days or so. This limited ability is both a blessing and a curse. The additional brain space occupied by long-term memory can be used for other, more important tasks, like identifying which types of dirt are best for making tea."

"Wait. Did you say you make tea from dirt? And do you call yourselves Malterns?"

The beast reared back on its log again. "Oocka, oocka, oocka! You humans have so many questions. You are an inquisitive species, aren't you? But yes, finding soil with the right composition of decayed plants and organic matter is a science among us. Travis, my elder cousin Maltern, is what we call a dirt-spotter and has a knack for finding the best tea grounds from, well, from the ground. Oocka, oocka, oocka!"

The beast was clearly amused by its joke. Its laughter made Michael pause again and realize how similar these creatures were to his own species, yet they still had their own unique personalities. If there was one thing he had never expected from all his past interests and suspicions about their existence, it was that they would have a sense of humor. They seemed gentle enough, and this new wrinkle of humor gave him an appreciation for their sophistication.

"Would you like to try some of my tea?"

Not wanting to offend the creature, Michael said, "Sure, thank you."

The beast stood and went to the far end of the hut and prepared the tea. As it did, Michael looked around and admired the construction of the hut. It appeared to be tightly strung together and solidly built, with a small chimney at the top for venting smoke.

The Maltern returned and handed Michael his tea in a quarter-full insulated Yeti mug. The beast held a handmade wooden cup of his own. "I'm sorry it's not heated; I don't have a fire at the moment."

"Thank you. No worries at all. I have to ask, where did you get the Yeti mug?" Michael asked, smiling at the irony. He thought for a moment about explaining the reference to Yetis being the legendary Bigfoot of the Himalayas and then decided against it. He'd already insulted his host with the Bigfoot moniker.

"Oh, that?" it said. "I got it from the landfill. You humans throw away the most functional things. Mountains of garbage! What is with that?"

"Well, in our society, we use currency to buy things. Because some items are so affordable, we dispose of them after we tire of them or upgrade to a newer item. It's horrible, I know," Michael explained.

The beast tilted its head again in a look of curiosity. "Seems wasteful and short-sighted to me, but okay. We held a council meeting regarding the looting of landfills and determined that, to keep our culture pure, each house could take only one item of significance from the landfill. I chose that mug mostly because it's functional. Of course, we are allowed to take as many books as we can—they are the one exception. We need to stay literate."

Michael sipped his tea, which, despite its heavy earthy notes, wasn't half bad.

"The tea is quite nice. So, I have to ask, what do you eat? How do you maintain that svelte Maltern figure?" Michael said, with a bit of snark in his voice.

"Oh, we eat a lot of foraged greens, ferns, mosses, and the like. It keeps us regular, that's for sure. Oocka, oocka, oocka!" The beast's fur shook from the weight of its laughter. "But seriously, greens and the occasional rabbit we snare or deer we might take down. Meat is scarce, but when we get it, we make a point of cooking it with some of the tastiest mushrooms we can find."

"Very interesting."

Michael paused for a second, then smiled and said with a bit of a laugh, "I'm sorry. I'm sitting here thinking no one out in the world would believe I had an actual conversation about food, drink, and culture with a Sasquatch who can read. Oh, sorry. I mean, a Maltern. It's just so far-fetched."

"Why is that so far-fetched?"

"Well, I mean, none of us humans ever thought your species could speak, let alone so eloquently. Furthermore, there is a basic assumption given your size and appearance: if you existed, you must be a terrifying, fearsome, and aggressive beast."

The Maltern stared forlornly at Michael for an uncomfortably long time. After a few seconds, Michael could see its eyes well up with tears. *Could this thing actually be crying?* He was stunned to think this big, hairy creature could have such powerful emotions.

"I'm sorry. Was it something I said?" Michael asked.

The beast wiped one eye, then the next, looked at Michael, and said, "Why would humans assume that about us based strictly on our appearance? That seems fairly shallow."

"I'm sorry I said that. I guess it's just that the human race has been classifying and pigeonholing people who don't look like themselves for centuries. As you say, it's horribly shallow, and in our case, has caused many wars over the years."

"As long as you mention wars, as you can see, I'm reading *Slaughterhouse Five*. I am wondering if the devastating fire-storming at Dresden really happened. Could something that horrible be true?" the beast asked.

"I'm afraid so. That and far worse things. There were two atomic bombs dropped on Japan that would make Dresden look like a campfire. Between them, over 200,000 people were killed."

Again, the beast's eyes teared up. He dropped his head into his hands and began sobbing uncontrollably. Michael stood up, walked over, and put his arm around the broad, hairy shoulders of the beast. As he held him, he lowered his head onto the shoulder and rested it there in a show of comfort.

Eventually, the beast gathered itself and raised its head again. "I'm sorry I lost control. It's just that we Malterns have never known such hatred and violence. I hope you realize how traumatizing it is to think about the deaths of so many humans. My brothers and sisters would have a tough time understanding how you could permit it to happen."

The beast's reaction reminded Michael that humans have found new ways and new wars to kill each other since the evolution of man. To think an "uncivilized" beast population wouldn't even entertain the idea hit Michael like a ton of bricks. Who were the truly civilized ones?

"I know. I know. All I can do is work against the violence and injustices and encourage others to do the same, right?"

"I guess so. But do you see now why we remain elusive creatures?"

"I do. I understand much better than when we first met." Michael paused. "Hey, I do have to get going. I have many miles yet to cover. But I have enjoyed our meeting. You have taught me much," Michael said.

The beast stood up. "I agree. And you have taught me as well. I would ask you never to mention this encounter to anyone, however. It would mean my entire species would be hunted down in these woods and either wiped out or forced to leave our homelands."

Michael nodded. "Yes, you have my word. This will forever remain our little secret."

"Of course, I too will keep our encounter to myself. It would only invoke fear and dread among my species."

"I understand. I will be going then."

"It was nice meeting you. Thank you again for the book. I can't wait to read it!" The beast spread its arms out and hugged Michael with crushing, loving strength. Michael was enveloped in the pungent, organic stench of the beast's fur from years of living in the outdoors but returned the affection as man and beast shared a moment.

The beast led Michael out the door and directed him back toward the main trail he had strayed from to bring him to this place. Michael thanked him and waved as he moved up the trail. As he hiked in the drizzle among the low-lying ferns and towering Douglas Firs, his thoughts were consumed by his experience with the gentle creature. What struck him most was the heightened sense of emotional sensitivity that seemed to be the modus operandi of the beast and its kind. Despite the Maltern's ominous size and imposing presence, he was as gentle as a lamb. It became glaringly apparent that most humans could stand to learn a thing or two from this species.

Michael knew he could never tell a soul about what had just happened. No, this legend must continue to stay as a legend.

He reached into his pack, grabbed a handful of trail mix, and, with a smile, popped it in his mouth and hiked ahead.

Priceless

Mark and Reggie were best friends from the neighborhood. In middle school, the ten-year-olds shared many of the same classes, both loved sports, and even had crushes on a couple of the same girls. Mark was a stocky kid with a constant summertime sweaty mop of brown hair. Kids at school teased him about his size, and when he confided in his parents, they reassured him he was fine for his age–just big-boned. In contrast, Reggie was gangly and thin. He could eat whatever he wanted and never gain an ounce, and was more meticulous about his appearance, especially his hair.

On a sultry June day in 1971, the two met up and made their way to the Corner Grocery, a small neighborhood store three blocks from Reggie's house. They both had their weekly allowances and were looking to blow the works on penny candy and football cards. It was one of the many summer activities when days were long and filled with endless possibilities. Trips to the store for cards and candy were sprinkled alongside others like fishing at the river, pickup baseball or just shelling sunflower seeds while listening to the transistor radio in the local church parking lot.

The tiny store was a mecca of sugar-coated crack hits for kids like Mark. The counter near the register was stocked with every conceivable candy. Bit O Honey, Dots, Charms suckers, Pop Rocks, Charleston Chews, and a seemingly endless horizon of penny candy. Mark picked out a few sweets and bought a couple of packs of football cards. The beauty of buying sports cards was not only the chance of getting some of your favorite team's players in a pack but also the stale piece of gum you always got to shove in your mouth while reading sports statistics on the back of each card. The two friends had taken to collecting and trading them. Mark was a faithful diehard Viking fan, and Reggie was, for some unknown reason, a Packer fan. The two freely swapped players from each of those teams, in part because they both knew what it meant to have their heroes in their collections. These cardboard treasures were part of who they were.

"Got an Alan Page card here, dude!" Reggie exclaimed.

"For real? Lemme see," Mark insisted.

Reggie handed him the card. Sure enough, there was number eighty-eight with his trademark short afro and purple and gold jersey. If there were a Viking player Mark would call his favorite, it would have to be Page. He was a dominant lineman and made up a quarter of the Purple People Eaters—the famous defensive front four of the Vikings.

"Dude, what do you want for him? I'll give you anything I've got."

"You can just have him. He means more to you than to me. Tell you what, if you get a John Brockington sometime, I'll take it," Reggie replied.

"Deal. Thanks! I've been waiting for this card for a year."

It was difficult for Mark to contain his joy at his newly acquired treasure. Getting his hands on this gem was an endorphin rush that fueled his love of the hobby. The holy grail of his sports card collection had finally come into his hands. Every card he collected from there on out was just gravy. Unless, of course, he got another Alan Page card. A duplicate would make his prize twice as relevant.

Acquiring it fueled his obsession even more. Unlike Reggie, who sometimes used some of his castoff cards in the spokes of his bike, Mark wouldn't treat any of his with such disrespect, regardless of who graced the picture. He knew in his heart each player was trying his best and any of them could become a star someday. He treated the cards like prized possessions.

Years later, in 2001, Reggie and Mark were together at a sports card show. Reggie had abandoned his collection shortly after entering high school, but Mark was still an avid collector. When they arrived at the exhibit hall at the State Fair Park, it was electric with activity. There were close to fifty vendor tables, most stocked with similar-looking displays featuring cards, jerseys, bats, balls, and other memorabilia. Hobbyists browsed and chatted with the sellers, sometimes haggling over prices and alleged values. Collectors and sellers both know the card market is volatile and capable of wild swings up and down depending on the state of the economy.

Mark determined early in his collecting days it wasn't about the money. It wasn't about investing or saving for the future. He did all of it for the love of sports, both the game and the people who played it. He was brutally aware most collectors had a bottom line in mind, but to him, it was all about possession. About owning things other people didn't. A complete set of 1974 Topps football cards? He had it. Signed helmet from Fran Tarkenton? It was his. His hobby filled a hole in his life that he wasn't even aware he had. It gave him a satisfaction nothing else could. When people commented about his obsession, he always replied, "It could be worse. It could be drugs." That usually shut them down.

"Holy cow! I didn't know what to expect, but this is over the top. Insane!" Reggie said as they entered the hall.

"Yeah, these are my people. I love the smell of cardboard in the morning," Mark replied.

"You're still big into this memorabilia thing, aren't you?"

"Yeah, I sorta am."

After a few minutes of wandering the aisles, Reggie bluntly said, "You know, these people are obsessed and crazy. You realize that, don't you?"

"I don't know, maybe. But to me, they're just really enthusiastic about their hobby. Like a guitarist who owns twelve guitars. The only thing more important than those is the thirteenth one he wants."

"Huh. I kinda get it, but to me, it's still mind-blowing that people get this involved with something as silly as pictures on cardboard."

"Well, you know, I always say it could be worse. It could be drugs."

"Ha! Yeah, you got me there."

As they walked along, it was never more than a few steps before Mark was chatting with one of the vendors. They talked about Ken Griffey Jr. rookie cards, a bat signed by Pete Rose, and, of course, whether they had any Alan Page cards for sale. He was up to twenty-three in his collection and was always looking to add to the pile.

By the time they left two hours later, Mark had purchased thirteen football box sets, two autographed baseball jerseys, and two of the original seats taken from the old Metropolitan Stadium before it was razed to make room for the Mall of America.

Loading the seats into Mark's SUV was tricky, but luckily, he'd kept some bungy cords in it for just this purpose. Once it was loaded, they got in the car.

"Man, your house isn't that big, Mark. Where are you going to put these seats?"

"Don't worry. I have the perfect place. Besides, they are pieces of sports history. Do you know how many nail-biting pitching duels have been witnessed from these seats? They were part of the agony behind every Fred Cox missed field goal or Chuck Foreman fumble. They gave people the chance to see coaching greats like Billy Martin and Bud Grant. Hell, they were even there for the Eagles, Steve Miller, and Pablo

Cruise concert in '78! I think if you sit in them and close your eyes, you will probably be able to hear 'Hotel California.'"

Reggie gave Mark a side-eye. "Whoa, dude. I wouldn't go that far, but okay…"

"Seriously, Reggie. These things speak to me, or at least to my soul. Collectibles are my thing, and they are like family and friends to me," Mark said defensively.

"Well, judging from the crowd, the ladies don't dig them like you do. How's the dating life going, by the way?"

"Not great at the moment. I had a couple of dates with Charlene, but she kept mocking my Minnesota sports wall of fame. Said it looked like something that should be in a kid's bedroom, so fuck her."

"You have a wall of fame in your house?"

"Sure. Of course, it's not as nice as some I've seen."

"You mean other people do this too?"

"Well, yeah! What's wrong with that?" Mark asked.

"Oh, nothing. No offense intended. I just think it's a weird thing to do in your house. But to each his own, I guess."

"Look, Reggie, do you have pictures of family around your house?"

"Yeah. I have one of my parents in the living room and even have a picture of Angela on my nightstand."

"Well, this wall is like that. My wall is my Angela."

"Okay, dude. Whatever. Now I have to see this wall of fame."

"Alright, before I drop you off at the Grand Tavern to get your car, I'll let you in to have a peek at it."

Mark pulled into the driveway, and the two of them got out and unloaded the car. Reggie was stunned when he walked into Mark's house. The entire living room was decked out with sports memorabilia. The walls were covered with pennants, old sports posters, and banners. One wall held a portion of an old scoreboard, complete with a few burned-out bulbs. The walls were painted Viking purple and complemented by gold curtains. The curtain pulls even had plastic Viking helmet emblems.

End tables and windowsills were stacked with items: signed 8×10 photos, bobblehead figurines, and autographed balls from all sports displayed in acrylic cases. Bookshelves were stuffed with sports biographies and back issues of Sports Illustrated. A pair of boxing gloves hung from the on/off chain of the ceiling fan. On the coffee table sat a purple foam brick with the words "Bad Call Brick" embossed on it. It served the intense sports fan's way of taking out their aggression on referees during games by chucking it harmlessly at the television screen.

They weaved their way between a few unopened boxes of collectibles to get to the dining room. The main wall was painted with wide vertical stripes. Purple and gold for the Vikings, blue and red for the Twins, and green and gold for the now-defunct North Stars hockey franchise. The wall was covered from ceiling to waist level with framed athlete pictures featuring stars from their respective sports. To add to the gaudiness, a bloodied mouthguard sat in an acrylic case on a shelf in the hockey section. A pair of well-worn cleats hung from a hook in the baseball portion, and what looked like a dirty towel hung in the football area.

"Holy criminy, Mark. This is wild."

"You like it? That mouthguard is from the famous North Stars/Bruins brawl of '81. A record 406 penalty minutes were issued in that game."

"I'll be honest with ya, man, it's kinda gross to have a mouthguard in your dining room. But maybe that's just me."

"Actually, no, it's not just you. Charlene said the same thing. Fuck Charlene!"

"Ha, ha. Yeah, fuck Charlene. Fairweather hockey fan. What's with the towel?"

"Oh, that? A player threw it to me as they were walking into the locker room at the last Vikings game at the Met. I didn't get his number, but just knowing the sweat of one of my heroes is in the fibers of it and that it came from that memorable last game, well, it's kinda priceless."

"Yeah, nothing says fine dining like the sweat of an athlete hanging on the wall."

"Shut up, man. Like I said, it's my gig. Leave me alone."

"I'm just giving you shit, Mark. This is actually pretty impressive."

The two made their way back out to Mark's car. Mark dropped Reggie at his car, and when he got back home, he spent the next two hours putting the complete sets he'd purchased in numerical order by card number. As he worked, he replayed the conversations with Reggie in his head. Some of Reggie's comments about his hobby stung to the core. It hurt that his words reinforced what Charlene and all the other women had said—his passion for collectibles was over-the-top.

I don't give a damn what they all think. This is who I am. Love it or leave it.

When he was tired of sorting, he went to the refrigerator and got a beer. He came out to the living room, turned off all the lights, and flicked on the scoreboard. It was a stadium artifact he'd seen at an auction; the portion showed the scores of other baseball games around the league. This one displayed BOS 6 and NYY 4 in stacked letters. In Mark's world, Boston won every night 6-4 over the Yankees. He hated the Yankees, so the sign was beloved.

Mark pushed the foldable seat down on one of the new stadium seats. They were numbered fifteen and sixteen. The seller had no idea where in the stadium they had originally sat, but it didn't matter to Mark. Not knowing where it had come from made dreaming about the possibilities even better. Maybe he'd sat in this very seat at one of the many Twins games he'd seen with his dad when he was young. It was almost certainly occupied by a screaming teenage girl at the only Beatles concert ever in Minnesota in 1965. Maybe a dignitary had sat in it during the Twins' 1965 World Series.

Mark realized this was what drove his love of collectibles. The memories they stirred, the possibilities each item held, the history stored within each book, each card, each program. He wouldn't go as far as to say the stuff talked to him, but he wouldn't deny that occasionally he heard whispers from it. The clutch strikeout, the cheer of the crowd, even the squeaky organ so commonplace at old stadiums before multi-megawatt sound systems took over. Mark couldn't help but laugh a little at himself and his thoughts. Maybe this was the start of a mental illness. He preferred to think he was simply a man with a passion, like Elvis and his car collection. He tipped back the last of his beer, got up, and toddled off to bed.

Mark came home from work, exhausted after a long day of programming for Synthcom Coders. It was the perfect job for an introvert like him. He loved working alone, and the logic behind coding had always come easy to him. At sixty, though, he was finding it hard to keep up with the young talent Synthcom had been hiring lately. Most new hires were talented coders, much younger than him.

When he opened the door to the house, he was surprised to hear silence instead of the raucous barking of Shaq, his Jack Russel/Beagle mix. Mark adopted him from the Humane Society last year to keep him company and found that he really appreciated having the dog around. It gave the place a new sense of life. While his sports heroes surrounded him, they were inanimate, frozen in time. Shaq had boundless energy, and he and Mark had created a bond only a dog owner could appreciate.

He was a chewer too. He'd gotten into one of Mark's 1971 box sets and chewed several of the cards beyond recognition. Mark had fumed and seethed for hours afterward but didn't lay a finger on Shaq. He was just a dumb dog, doing what came naturally. It was a lesson for Mark to put things up out of the dog's reach.

"Shaq? Here, boy," he called out.

More silence. He went into the kitchen. No sign of him there. His vintage 1958 Snoopy food and water dishes Mark had picked up on eBay were in their usual spot, but no dog. He went to the dining room—nothing out of order there. His anxiety spiked.

It was when he entered the bedroom that he found Shaq. He was lying on the floor lifeless, tongue hanging out. Mark rushed over and kneeled.

"Shaq! Wake up, Shaq!" He ran his hand over the dog's head and felt a large bump. It was then he saw the Earl Anthony autographed bowling pin lying a short distance from Shaq. For years, it had sat undisturbed on the top shelf of his bookcase, along with a Dick Weber bowling ball and two signed football helmets. With Shaq's propensity for climbing and getting into things, it looked like the pin had toppled and struck Shaq on his head. It must have hit just right because the dog was clearly dead and had been for a while.

"No, no! This can't be happening. Shaq, no! No, no, no…" His words fell into tears as he cradled the dog and rocked back and forth.

After ten rings, the phone went to Mark's voicemail. It was the fourth time in two days for Reggie, who'd been trying to contact him. Despite the messages he'd left, Mark hadn't called back. Nor had he mentioned going out of town when they were together at Champs sports bar just last week. They'd gotten together for a couple of beers and to watch the Twins game on the big screen. The conversation had been superficial, about sports and work issues. At some point in the conversation, they had talked about a few mutual friends who had passed away in the past few years. They were both in their early sixties; these deaths were hitting close to home, and Mark seemed especially distraught for some reason.

"We are of a certain age now, man. Nothing is guaranteed anymore," Mark had said with a laugh.

"That's the truth," Reggie agreed.

"You've gotta appreciate every day, buddy. Go out and get what you've always wanted. Take me, for instance. Last week I bought a copy of the Marilyn Monroe Playboy issue from 1953 for two grand. That's a steal, given its condition. I wanted it. I'm sixty-two, and now it's mine. Done," Mark had said, hammering home his point.

"Yeah, and just appreciate time with your family and friends, like we are right now," Reggie added.

"Yes sir. That too."

It was nice to have a lifelong friend like Mark, so Reggie was a little concerned when he couldn't contact him by phone. He decided to check in.

He parked on the street and strode up the front walk. Mark's car was parked outside the garage, which usually meant he was at home. Despite his infatuation with sports, Mark was wildly out of shape. He wasn't really a walker and didn't own a bike, so he was probably inside watching sports or something.

Reggie rang the doorbell and waited. Nothing. He rang again, then knocked for good measure and still got no answer. The drapes were drawn, which seemed odd for the middle of the day. Reggie saw a small gap between the drapes in the window and took a peek.

As he peered into the living room, his jaw dropped. The entire room was stacked with boxes, Rubbermaid totes, and newspapers. Furniture was covered with stuff, including trophies, jerseys, and other memorabilia. Though he and Mark were still friends, they'd been pulled in separate directions over the years. They'd gotten together a few times over those years, but always at a bar. Reggie hadn't been to his house since the card show twenty years ago.

"What the…?" He returned to the front door and turned the knob. The door was unlocked, but when he pushed it, it was blocked. He looked down to see stacks of detritus two feet high, which were blocking the door from fully opening. He put his shoulder into it, and it gave way to open six inches. It was enough to get his head in and validate his earlier discovery. The entire living area was covered with boxes. Despite looking like a hoarding situation, there weren't any food containers and garbage. There was, however, a definite funk in the air that caused his urgency to ramp up. It was clear he couldn't get in, so he went around to the back.

Reggie looked into the kitchen through the door window. "Oh, no!"

He tried the door and found it also to be unlocked. He pushed it open and rushed over to his friend. Mark's body was slumped over his breakfast. His face was firmly planted in the bowl of Wheaties he had been eating. Reggie saw that the front of the box had the 1987 Minnesota Twins in a hog pile, a collectible box from their World Series victory so long ago. Next to the table was a Rubbermaid tote with twelve more unopened boxes of cereal.

Could he really have been eating cereal from 1987? It's no wonder he's dead.

Mark was dressed in an autographed Fran Tarkenton jersey with red and blue Twins Zubaz pants, a throwback to the nineties that should have been left there. Reggie felt Mark's neck for a pulse. Nothing. Tears formed in his eyes at the thought of losing his lifelong friend. They fell as he broke down and sobbed incessantly. When he pulled himself together, he noticed on the kitchen table, in a small arc around Mark's slumped body, were trophies for basketball, baseball, and even women's bowling. Reggie looked at a couple, and while some were from Mark's boyhood days; others were clearly not. One read "Second Place, Women Seniors 2001 Tournament, Sandusky, Ohio."

Why would a person buy someone else's trophy, let alone display it?

Reggie pulled out his phone and dialed 911. When he was finished, he took a walk through the house. Every room was stacked with boxes and Rubbermaid totes full of collectible memorabilia, each of them labeled with its contents. The boxes and totes formed narrow aisles that led to each room.

As Reggie got to Mark's bedroom, it caused a start. On Mark's dresser was an 8×10 photo of Reggie in his Cincinnati Reds Little League uniform. It was flanked on either side with pictures of the two of them at Twins and Viking games. In front of it were a couple of votive candles. Despite the obvious memorabilia hoarding situation, Reggie was touched by the sentimentality of his friend. Mark had never married, and this shrine made it obvious his relationship with Reggie was dear to him.

The congregation gathered at the local Methodist church a few blocks from Mark's house. Reggie had heard the coroner's report had ruled his death to be from a cerebral aneurysm. Mark had lived with high blood pressure for years, and it had finally caught up with him. Reggie was grateful that at least the event was quick and painless, albeit less than dignified—face down in a bowl of ancient Wheaties.

Mid-service, Reggie stepped up to the pulpit to say a few words about his friend. He looked out at the crowd, most of them dressed in sports jerseys of one type or another. The attire was a request to friends and family from Mark's elderly mother in recognition of his love of sports. Reggie gathered himself and began.

"Mark was the best friend a guy like me could ask for. He was always quick with a laugh and would give his right arm for friends and family.

"And while he led a beautiful life, much of it in solitude by choice, Mark's life was the manifestation of a hobby gone bad. His love for sports and collectibles started when we were kids collecting football cards we got at the local grocery. By the time of his death, his house was overcome with boxes of collectibles.

"But understand, I do not fault him for this or hold him in judgment. Each and every one of those thousands of items meant something to him. I sincerely believe that. On several occasions, he told me the memories some of the things evoked: the last-second goal, the athletic accomplishments of the star of the team, or the euphoria of the game-winning field goal. While some folks find their love in people or relationships, or in hobbies like fishing and reading, Mark found his in tangible items tied to sports heroes and teams, which gave his life purpose.

"It can best be summed up in what he once said when I commented about his crazy love for collectibles. He said, 'Reggie, sometimes people like different things.' It was a statement that swayed me from judgment to enlightenment. It can be applied across the spectrum of our life experiences. Everything from travel to art and literature and really anything in this life. In Mark's case, it was hobbies. Mark liked different things. Once you understand this basic life premise, you can more genuinely love people where they are. More importantly, this acceptance and grace will make your life infinitely more beautiful. So…thank you, dear friend, for that advice. May you rest in peace."

The congregation broke out in thunderous applause. It went on for a few seconds and before long, they stood, raising their arms and doing the wave—a favorite activity of fans everywhere during baseball games.

Ethangora

Jacob's move to the Pacific Northwest came shortly after college. He'd heard good things about the region and wanted to get away from the Upper Midwest. Jacob grew up in Stevens Point, Wisconsin, and, after getting a degree in Environmental Studies from the university there, he needed more than city life could offer. He longed to be closer to the natural wonders, coasts, and wildness of states like Oregon and Washington. His move to Eugene, Oregon, in 2021 was life changing. While Jacob certainly missed his family and friends back home, his life among the gigantic trees, magnificent waterfalls, and craggy coastal areas of Oregon took his mind off his home two thousand miles to the east.

Jacob was working at Spearhead Technologies as a geographic information systems analyst in Eugene. It provided some broad experience in a field he was growing to love. Much of his project work involved impact studies related to timber logging and other environmental analyses that complemented the focus of his undergraduate degree. While he understood logging was a necessary industry, he was also fiercely protective of trees. He loved to camp and fish, so his recreational pursuits fueled his career path in conservation and wildlife preservation.

Songs by The Gorillaz thumped from his car stereo as Jacob's black compact bent and groaned around the curves along the craggy Oregon coast. Every turn provided a vista more stunning than the previous. A soft, misty rain drifted down as the intermittent wipers cleared the windshield, providing moments of clarity and focus between passes. Huge basalt rocks thrust upward offshore, giving the coast a personality along with its jaw-dropping vistas.

These rocks told stories millions of years old. Stories of fire and volcanism, of intense heating and cooling, of change and renewal. Their history was as real to him as the rising of the sun each day. He wasn't sure if this reality was because of the courses he'd taken or if he had some innate connection with the earth that others didn't. Jacob smiled to himself as the thought passed through his mind. *Huh, like you think you're some sort of natural-world Buddhist monk or something.* Conversations with his id had come more frequently since he'd moved to Oregon, in part because he was alone so much. He trusted it was just part of a normal inner voice everyone has.

Jacob was headed south on Highway 101, high above the roiling Pacific. His destination lay across the border in Jedediah Smith Redwoods State Park. He was trekking there to hike among the towering trees. He'd seen his share of massive Douglas Firs in his brief time in Oregon, but it only made him crave for more, for bigger. Immersion into these natural environments provided a sense of calm and serenity that just wasn't possible in city living. Based on the research he'd done, he knew the redwoods would be a step or two above any majestic Doug Fir he'd seen, so he'd made the trip down to wander among them.

He pulled into the park and purchased a day pass using the drop box at the vacant entrance booth. The Civic purred down the winding highway into the park as the incredible stature of the trees came into view. His goal was the Grove of the Titans Trail. His online research mentioned it as one of the best trails in the park.

When he came to Howland Hill Road, he could hardly believe the GPS was leading him the right way. It was a narrow, rutted, often steep road, one better suited for an SUV than for his Civic; that much was sure.

"Wow!" he said aloud as he took in the magnitude of the trees. He knew talking aloud to himself was weird, but he couldn't help it. Trees with unfathomable trunks stretched and yawned skyward. They stood sentinel and towering, reminding him he and his little vehicle were small and insignificant in this cosmic and holy place. The car's hum seemed disruptive to the stifling quiet as Jacob piloted his way to the trailhead.

When he saw the sign for the Grove of Titans trail, he pulled over to a wide spot on the road and parked. There was no one else around on this Tuesday morning, which was fine with him. He loved his solitude, especially in the forest. He stepped out of the car and made his way to the trailhead. The air was heavy and humid, and the damp ground almost seemed to sweat. He looked skyward into a delicate luminescent fog drifting among the branches of the redwoods. The cloudy mist lingered there, providing hydration for thirsty boughs. Trees of this size needed plenty of water and here they took what was needed and gave back in respiration.

As he stepped down the trail, Jacob was overwhelmed by a sense of smallness. He'd been around skyscrapers in cities, but this was different. Way different. There was something about being among these giants thrusting from the earth that etched an imprint on his soul. Above him somewhere was the sun, but the tree canopy only allowed random shafts of light to slice through. Where it did, the low-lying ferns drank it like whiskey. Jacob wasn't a religious person, but he knew for sure if there was a God, He or She was certainly dwelling among these trees. "Thank you for all of this, God," he whispered.

"Tell me more about this God you speak of."

Jacob stopped in his tracks. He listened for a few seconds. *What the hell? Was that real?* He shook his head to clear it, attributing it to his inner voice, then continued walking.

"Human thing, who is 'God'?"

He stopped again. He'd heard it this time. It was a gruff, gravelly whisper of a voice, but one he could not dismiss as being in his head. He'd definitely heard it with his ears. Determined to see if it was real, he answered in a low voice, "Who said that?"

"It is We and Us, all of my family, human thing."

"Uh, okay. And who's "we"?"

"I asked you first, who is this God?" Jacob spun around and looked deep into the trees to see if there was someone hidden away playing some sort of weird trick on him. Nothing. He answered, "Well, from what I was taught, God created everything. It is said that God cannot be described."

"Hmmm. Sounds more like Ethangora to We and Us." There was a momentary whisper of wind among the branches that shivered overhead. It almost seemed like the trees all around him were acknowledging what was just said.

"So, I told you who God is; now, who are you and what is 'Ethangora'?" Jacob said quietly to the apparent spirit speaking to him.

"We are Us and Us are We. We are the trees, but we stand not alone. For without the dirt within which we stand, we are nothing. Without the ferns shading our roots, we are lonely wooden shells. Without the animals, insects, birds, fungi, and even the moss, we are not *we*, but *I*. And *Ethangora* has no time for *I*."

Jacob stood there dumbly. *Am I losing my mind? Trees just don't talk.* He walked on but continued the conversation.

"So Ethangora is your god, then?"

"Hmrr, hmrr, hmrr," the trees seemed to laugh. "No, human thing. It is more like the original form your god intended for humankind. Whereas human things were once intended to be part of We and Us, they instead have elevated themselves above the natural world. They now think of themselves as more dominant and set apart, and spend much of their energy consuming rather than coexisting. Ethangora originated from We and Us. It is the forest spirit but also an ethos, a system of beliefs and values. This ethos cannot stand above and apart from the forest. Rather, it must come from within We and Us. We and Us are on one earthly plane, all equal. Anytime there is a hierarchy, it leads to jealousy and a desire for power. All goodness comes from the corporate whole of We and Us, never from I."

Again, the trees shivered their agreement, a natural standing ovation.

When it quieted, the tree continued in its low, raspy voice, "Ethangora both guides us and *is* us. If it helps human things to understand, we came from Ethangora, which is life, and therefore We and Us are here to foster and nurture all of life. It is why we flourish in the diversity of our home, or ecosystem, as human things call it."

Jacob nodded his agreement. Throughout this conversation, he'd grown comfortable speaking to these sentinel beings, though couldn't help but feel he was learning something too. As he walked, it was apparent that his trail location meant nothing. The speech from the trees seemed to follow him along, maintaining its low, gruff voice as he traversed the undulating path through this holy cathedral in the woods. The forest as a whole enveloped him in its essence. For the first time in his life, he felt he was a welcome part of the ecosystem.

"Then what of fire? How do you and they perceive it and explain its threat? It certainly can't be sanctioned as good by Ethangora."

"That is a good question, human thing. We have lost many of We and Us to the power of fire. With all due respect, though, we have lost many more to the saws in the hands of human things. With fire, we stand together with a fighting chance. Many of We and Us have lived through fire, and yet, none touched by the saw have survived. Fire has its purpose in Ethangora, but saws only kill for killing's sake. There is no goodness in its teeth, only death."

"You do realize I love nature and studied it in school. I could never cut down a tree," Jacob said in his defense.

"But you humans think not of We and Us. Only of I. Do you all not possess the same desire to kill and conquer?"

"No, we do not. That is where we differ from you and they. While your essence is centered on goodness for the whole, we humans have that as well as a powerful pull for I. I succumbs to greed, power, and selfishness. I often surfaces and takes over. Wars were fought for I. Marriages between two people are wrecked by I. People are hurt by I. Come to think of it, anytime I comes before we, not much good comes from it."

"Pfh, pfh, pfh." A light mist began breaking through the canopy. Jacob wasn't sure, but it almost sounded like the trees were crying. Crying for the selfishness of humanity, like we were the ones in need of enlightenment. The forest air suddenly hung heavy with sadness.

"You are wise for your young age, human thing. We and Us have been honored to speak with you today. You need to continue your journey to truth and symbiotic unity. We and Us will leave you to enjoy the rest of your time in our home, observing silence. We and Us wish you peace and contentment during your time on this magnificent and fragile Earth. Your time here is short compared to ours. Use it wisely. Remember the essence of Ethangora. May you see it in everything you encounter here forward."

With that, the trees fell silent.

"Wait, are you still there?"

The sweeping boughs of the trees only whispered in the misty breeze of the Pacific Coast.

Fender Bender

Willie's fretwork cut searing notes on Agatha, his prized Fender Stratocaster. His fingers moved fluidly, with skill and mastery. He bent the strings to carry the notes to new places, resonating from the Marshall amplifier out to the small crowd gathered at Anodyne Coffee in Milwaukee. It seemed a paltry crowd, but he was grateful for anyone who showed up to hear him, especially on a cold Wednesday in November. For a part-time guitar and vocalist hack in his early fifties, he played pretty well. His music crossed three genres: blues, country, and rock, all of which could be played with a single guitar, kicking amp, and good set of pedals. Most of his love was for the electric guitar, but he also used a six-string Gibson acoustic to keep his repertoire fresh.

His preference of electric over acoustic stemmed in part from the Stratocaster itself. The guitar was signed by John Lee Hooker and Bonnie Raitt, and Willie had named it Agatha. It was the name of an old girlfriend he'd never quite gotten over. He was a big fan of B.B. King who named his guitar Lucille, so Willie thought he'd do the same and name his. It would help him carry memories of Agatha with him through the years. His friend Stephon booked bands for venues in the Milwaukee circuit and occasionally had inside connections to get backstage passes for shows. When he hooked Willie up with one for John Lee

Hooker at a small club in Milwaukee, and Bonnie Raitt for a gig at Summerfest, he lugged his guitar with him in hopes of an autograph. Both stars were gracious about it and scrawled their names in low-contact areas of the guitar body.

The Stratocaster whined and howled as he sang.

"Judith Lee keeps showing up around here,
breathin' fireworks and smoke and flames.
She eats all my food and drinks all my beer
and keeps on rollin' just the same."

Willie's music was built around a life he'd never known. He had a knack for writing about the rambling, traveling lives of lost souls, drunks, and vagabonds. His songwriting allowed him to go to distant places in the country without ever leaving the state. He was a dyed-in-the-wool local. Born and raised in Milwaukee, he never ventured too far from southeastern Wisconsin. Some of his shows took him to La Crosse and Green Bay, but they were the exception. He preferred the local Milwaukee and suburbs scene.

When Willie was young, his parents dragged him back and forth across Wisconsin to Hudson on holidays to see his grandparents. Between the smothering cigarette smoke and the nauseating sway of the Olds Delta 88, he'd puked his guts out with bouts of car sickness on several occasions. His parents' twisted way of dealing with it was to bring a generous supply of plastic bags and tell him to use them as needed so they wouldn't have to stop. These death trips of his youth had stripped away any love of travel for him. Even in adulthood, his thought was, *the less driving, the better.* Willie liked the familiarity of home best.

Willie met Jaime while they were both attending the University of Wisconsin-Milwaukee. She was an attractive, willowy blonde with a warm smile and a girl-next-door charm about her. The two had started young and hopelessly in love. He majored in communications and she was a linguistics grad. They married eight months after graduating, and for the first several years, they were smitten. She came to some of his gigs—mostly minor affairs in backroom bars, but occasionally bigger venues like a side stage at Summerfest.

However, not everything was perfect between them. His drinking was a constant sore spot for her. Willie grew up with a father who was a drinker with a temper. He'd never told Willie he loved him, and on nights he was on his benders, he was a mean cuss to both his wife and his son. Willie's insecurities about his self-worth and his self-esteem led him to a drinking problem of his own. He differed from his father in that he was a happy drunk, but a drunk just the same. When he played the bars, liquor was always around, and for him as a musician, it was usually free. He'd regularly come home wasted on those nights when Jaime wasn't at his show. She suspected he was drinking more at home on nights she had to work, as he was often asleep when she got home from working at the restaurant at 9:30.

Bigger than the drinking issue, though, was their disagreement over travel. Jaime longed to get out of Wisconsin and see the country. Willie was evasive about the subject and kept telling her to make a girls' trip out of it.

"I don't want to travel with them. I want to do it with you. You know that whole build-your-life-together thing we agreed on at the altar? Yeah, that."

Willie stood his ground despite her sarcasm and occasional zingers. She never understood his dislike of long drives, and it became another unfortunate source of tension between them. Eventually, their differences ended in an amicable split, which Willie chalked up to one of those curveballs life throws at you sometimes. He'd written a song about it titled "Done Burnt Down," which pretty much tells it all.

Willie's reverb hung in the air for a few seconds as he finished out the set. The crowd clapped in approval, including a few whistles and hoots. He'd played gigs at the Blues Estate on the east side of Milwaukee and always appreciated the crowds that patronized the place. They were true hip music buffs who could relate to his musical wandering across the various genres. A small but musically cultured following.

He took off his guitar, set it on the stand in the wings of the stage, and headed to the bar. While he loved performing, there was a part of him that loved the post-performance celebrations almost as much.

"Hey Cristina, can I get a whiskey sour?" he asked. Cristina was girl-next-door cute and had a sass to her that fit the bartending role well.

"You got it, Willie."

Cristina poured heavy-handed drinks for the regulars, especially the musical guests. For her, the sour in a whiskey sour was strictly for color. She'd seen Willie close the place enough to know he could take what she delivered. Four cocktails later, as midnight approached, she started closing up. Willie was pleasantly buzzed and made his way over to pack up his equipment. These endings were his least favorite part of playing gigs. It meant returning to his reality, his job at his landscaping company.

After graduating, he'd discovered there weren't a lot of jobs for a communications degree, so he started landscaping to see if he could be his own boss. He built up the business over the years, picking up equipment and even an employee—Nate—as his customer base grew. What he'd once enjoyed had lately become a drain, and he was looking for what was next. Willie was a lost soul—a divorced lost soul at that—much like the characters he'd sung about for the last twenty years.

With the car all packed with his guitar and equipment, Willie took the less-traveled streets back to his house in Greenfield. He knew the routes the cops patrolled and wanted to stay under the radar. So, he drove like a grandma and, like he'd done many times after gigs, he breathed a sigh of relief when he pulled into his driveway. Drunk and tired, he hauled himself into his house and fell into bed.

The next morning, he woke up to someone pounding on his door. His head thumped and sloshed as he got out of bed and made his way toward the racket. He peeked through the door's small window and saw his neighbor Justin standing patiently. Willie opened the door. "Hey, Justin, what's up, man?"

Justin was relatively new to the neighborhood, having bought the bungalow next to him a few years prior.

"Hi, Willie. Sorry to bother you, buddy, but I wanted to let you know your car looks like it's been broken into. I came out to go to work and noticed your driver's side window was busted. I hope you had nothing of value in there," Justin said.

Willie's heart dropped as he craned his neck to see his car in the driveway. "What? Are you kidding me?"

Willie stepped out and started walking toward his car. As he approached it, he could see shards of safety glass littering the driveway. He looked in and saw the rest of his window peppering the floor and seat.

"Shit! My guitar!"

Whoever it was didn't care enough to steal his amplifier or his acoustic, but his prize Stratocaster was nowhere to be seen.

One week later, Willie got home from work at the usual six o'clock p.m. He pulled into his driveway, locked his car, and walked toward the front door. On the way in, he grabbed the mail. Three junk mailers from local businesses and one envelope, which was addressed in printed block letters. He walked into the house, tossed the mailers in the trash, and slid his finger to open the envelope.

In it was a picture of his guitar leaning up next to a bronze statue of a man holding an acoustic guitar. A sign on a post hung above that read, 'Standing on the Corner.' In the background was a building with a large marquee with the words Winslow, Arizona, in huge letters. Being a music nut, Willie quickly made the connection. He'd grown up listening to "Take It Easy" by the Eagles and knew of the statue, which served as a tourist attraction in downtown Winslow.

The note that accompanied the photo was also carefully printed and read:

Take it easy! The Eagle has landed and is a fine sight to see. If you're standing on the corner, there should be a clue tucked on the underside of the informational kiosk across the street. If you want your guitar back, that's a good place to start.

Willie stared at the note, perplexed. *What the heck?*

He re-read the note three times, then took a closer look at the photo to ensure it was Agatha. There was no doubt it was his as he saw the signatures on the body. After pondering the note for a couple of minutes, one thing became abundantly clear. He needed to go to Winslow.

The car stereo in the Kia Soul hammered out blues and rock hits from Willie's Spotify playlist as the miles rolled by. His first time in Iowa was nothing short of underwhelming. Nothing but the sight of corn and the occasional smell of hogs for miles and miles. Missouri wasn't much better but at least held the appeal of having Kansas City to see out the window for a short stretch. KC, home of the Super-Bowl-winning Chiefs and the subject of the famous song, "Kansas City." The hit is heavily covered by some of the blues greats and was one he'd played himself a few times at gigs. As he rolled past the city, he put the song on Spotify and belted out the verses. The lyrics mention getting there by trains and planes, but never a Kia, a fact that made him grin when he thought about it. It was nice finally putting a place to the song he'd sung.

It felt good to be tooling down the road and freed up some mind-space in away from the day-to-day craziness. November was a slow time between seasons at work, and he'd been able to get Nate to cover the existing jobs for as long as it took him to find the guitar. He hoped it wouldn't take more than a week to get it back home but was determined to follow the lead he'd gotten in the mail.

The ride provided him with time to think and reflect on the path he had traveled in life. When he crossed into the state of Kansas, he thought of the time he'd seen the band, Kansas, with his ex-wife Jaime at the Wisconsin State Fair. Then, a long, flat drive later at the Oklahoma line, he thought of the song "Oklahoma" from the musical of the same name. He never much liked musicals though, and for him, the state was as dull as the song. By evening, he was tired and stayed the night in a cheap motel in Guymon, Oklahoma, located almost dead center in the state's panhandle.

In the morning, he woke and hit the road following a quick breakfast in the motel lobby. After a long day in the car, he finally pulled into Winslow in the late afternoon. Willie parked his Kia Soul across the street from the famous statue downtown. Similar to thousands of tourists before him, he walked over to the monument and took a selfie in front of it.

He wandered over to the informational kiosk near the statue. The kiosk told of some of the lore about the corner reference from the song, as well as highlighting some of the city's local businesses and history. Willie tried to look nonchalant as he felt underneath the shelf for some kind of clue. On the underside of the third shelf he checked, he found an envelope taped to it. He pulled it off, put it in his pocket, and walked back to the car.

Inside the Soul, he opened the envelope. Like the previous note, it was printed in blue ink and had a photo with it.

The photo showed a picture of his guitar leaning against a small building, or more like a shack. Above the shack stood a sign: *A1 Keys*.

The note read:

> *You made it to the corner. Now you need to be like Arlo and get into Los Angeles. There, you can pick up a couple of keys at A1 Locksmith and Keys. Tell them Arlo sent you. That'll move you much closer to your guitar, provided you still want it.*

Willie made the connection right away to the Arlo Guthrie song, "Coming into Los Angeles." It seemed this person, this thief, had musical knowledge to go along with their warped sense of humor.

"Oh, my God, really?" Willie said aloud. "Los Angeles?"

His head spun at the idea of having to travel even farther. He'd never been to California, and he'd already seen more of the country than he'd ever dreamed. He even waffled for a moment, wondering if this goose chase across the country was still worth it. Then, the thought of his guitar being on the other end of it quickly erased the idea of giving up. He had to get it back.

Willie Googled motels in the area and decided to spend the night in Winslow. He would head out for Los Angeles in the morning, but at that moment, he needed a shower and a bed for the night.

Willie woke to a ray of sunlight cutting through a small slit between the drawn curtains in his motel. He'd slept fitfully but felt surprisingly rested and alert for 6:30, especially given the cruddy mattress he was on. He showered and ate a granola bar and a raspberry yogurt cup he'd bought the night before. When he was finished, he packed his bag. He threw open the curtains and was hit with the full, harsh sunbeams of Arizona. But what hit him more was what was not there, specifically, his Kia Soul.

"What the hell? Where's my car?" he said to no one.

He'd parked it right outside his room the night before, and now it was nowhere to be found. He opened the door, walked out to the parking spot, and looked around. There was some safety glass lying on the ground on what would have been the passenger side.

"Shit!"

He pulled out his cell phone and googled the Winslow Police Department to get a phone number. He dialed, and after a few rings, a woman answered. "Winslow Police Department, this is Marie. How can I help you?"

"Hi, my name is Willie Bradford. It appears my car has been stolen."

"I'm sorry to hear that, sir. Can you describe the vehicle and where you last saw it, and we'll look into it?"

"Yeah, it's a 2019 Kia Soul. It's silver, and I'm staying at the Best Western in town here. It was outside my motel last night at eight o'clock and was gone this morning."

Willie filled the dispatcher in with the rest of the details and information. They said they'd get back to him within an hour or two if they'd found anything. He hung up and sat on the edge of his bed. With nothing to do but sit and wait, he texted Nate back in Milwaukee.

Willie: *Dude, you won't believe what just happened. My car was stolen.*

Nate: *Wait, what? For real?*

Willie: *I kid you not. WTAF?*

Nate: *Man, that sucks. People suck.*

Willie: *They do. Anyway, I'll let you know what I hear. If I find it, I'm probably heading to LA.*

Nate: *LA? I thought your guitar was in Winslow.*

Willie: *Yeah, me too. Whoever it is has me on some sort of twisted music-based treasure hunt. Giving me clues from music lyrics and shit. I can't make this stuff up, man. Hopefully LA will get me a little closer to my guitar.*

Nate: *Of course, you'll need a car to get there…LOL.*

Willie: *Yeah, thanks for the reminder lol*

Thirty minutes later, Willie's phone jumped to life. He clicked and answered it. "Hello?"

"Hi, yes. Is this Mr. Bradford?"

"Yes, it is."

"This is Marie again from Winslow PD. We found your car. It was abandoned near the elementary school in town. They towed it to the impound lot where you can pick it up after you prove ownership."

"Okay, great news. Is it drivable?"

"I can't answer that, sir. Typically, these kinds of thefts are just joyrides for thrills and then abandoned. But I don't know its condition. You should come to the station and file a report, then retrieve the vehicle."

"Alright, I'll be there as soon as I can. I'll need to get a ride there, obviously," Willie said. He finished the call, hung up, and then called an Uber.

The Soul hurtled westward at 75 mph as Willie took in the desert landscape as seen through the windshield with thousands of miles of dirt and bugs behind it. Willie cracked all the windows to get rid of the cheap cologne and weed smell that permeated the inside. Whoever stole his car was apparently trying to neutralize the marijuana smell with their heavy layer of eau de toilette. It appeared they were smart enough not to sync their phone to Bluetooth which may have provided a trail to the thief.

He'd spent the better part of the morning retrieving the car from the impound lot and getting the broken window fixed. These intangibles from the trip were taking a toll on his bank account. Turns out they'd done a job on his steering column using a screwdriver and a USB charger to start the car. Willie knew the Kias were a popular target by car thieves for just this reason. Ease of access. The thief knew what they were doing. He had to hand it to them, the scum.

To pass the long hours through the desert, Willie added a playlist to Spotify featuring songs with lyrics about California. It cycled through songs like Zeppelin's "Going to California," John Hiatt's "Adios to California," and, of course, the Eagles' hit, "Hotel California." It was the music from the Eagles that started this whole quest, so that song seemed especially relevant. Willie was surprised at how many songs referenced California, and it piqued his interest as he sped across the state line.

The arid desert environment was so foreign to him as a person from the weather-beaten Midwest. While he missed the green landscape so prevalent in Wisconsin, he had to admit this was a pleasant change. The mountains and buttes so far off in the distance were something he'd never seen in anything but pictures and movies and were a nice diversion from flat and brown.

After long, boring hours on the expressway, he soon discovered the freneticism of Los Angeles traffic, and it made him twitchy and anxious. The last thing he needed was a car accident in a state thousands of miles from home. The traffic reminded him of the 80s song by Missing Persons, "Nobody Walks in LA." It sure seemed that way, and most of them were on the freeway, evidently.

He exited and wound his way through the city streets, following the commands coming from Google Maps. He pulled his car into a parking spot outside the A1 Keys and Locksmith shack. It sat on 3rd Street, a busy parkway. The structure was smaller than most people's garages. Willie got out and walked up to the shack.

A clerk wearing a collared shirt with the A1 logo on the pocket came to the window. "Can I help you?"

"Uh, yeah. This might sound strange, but someone told me you'd have a package for me. I'm looking for my guitar," Willie said.

"Oh, yeah. The guitar guy." The clerk reached under the counter and handed Willie a small box wrapped in brown paper.

"Do I owe you anything for it?" Willie asked.

"Nope. It was given to me by someone with instructions just to give it to you. I was told not to do anything more than that."

"So, you can't tell me who it was or what they looked like?"

"Sorry, man. They paid me nicely, and I gave them my word."

"Okay, well, I guess this will do for now. Thanks for your honesty," Willie said.

"No problem. Hope you find your guitar, buddy."

"Thanks, me too."

Willie took the package back to his car and opened it. Inside it were a key, a note, and a couple of pictures. He unfolded the note and read it.

> *If you're going to San Francisco, you don't need flowers in your hair to visit Saint Agnes, where there is no Haight. The third pew on the left. Psalm 33:2-3 should be enlightening in more ways than biblically. And I have to confess, the end is near!*

The first line immediately brought the Scott McKenzie song "San Francisco" to mind. One picture included with the note showed his guitar propped up against a Haight Street sign. The other had it leaning against the façade of a church, complete with Saint Agnes Catholic Church spelled out on a purple banner behind it.

"Aw, crap. San Francisco now? What the hell?" he said aloud. Here he had driven across the country, and now this petulant thief was playing musical geographic hide-and-go-seek games with him. He was tired of driving and just wanted to get back to his life in Milwaukee. At the same time, he realized he was seeing places he'd never seen before. One thing was sure; he would not drive all the way to San Francisco today. Willie wanted to see a little of the Hollywood area and some of the LA sites. He pulled out his phone, found a hotel near downtown, and made reservations.

The rest of the afternoon he spent seeing the places he'd seen only on television or in movies. He went to Venice Beach and people-watched for an hour. The beautiful sandy beach and cerulean-blue ocean all seemed so surreal to his Midwestern psyche. He drove to Beverly Hills and took a selfie by the sign for it and sent it to Nate. He did the same with the Hollywood sign. Nate was probably getting sick of his texts, but Willie couldn't help himself. It was so cool to be among these iconic and historic places.

Willie slipped into appreciation mode. It felt good to be away from everything familiar to him. He was surprised at how much he loved the unknowns of exploring. He wasn't ready to admit he was wrong for all the times he'd told Jaime he didn't like to travel, but he was beginning to understand what she saw in changing her surroundings by jumping in a car.

After the Hollywood sign shot, he found out where the Hollywood Bowl was and took a ride there. At a pullover on one hill, he got a view of it from above. A hint of jealousy fell over him as he thought of all the rock stars that had been on the stage. *Maybe someday I'll play it*, he laughed.

From there, he wound his way back down the mountain and made a trip to the Dolby Theatre. He walked down the Avenue of Stars, where many of the names drew him back to movies he'd seen. The sidewalk was crowded, bustling with vacationers mixed with California natives. He was shocked by how much he enjoyed the area, despite its pandering to tourists. LA wasn't as bad as people had made it out to be.

Early in the afternoon the next day, Willie made it to San Francisco. The ride to get there was a long line of fast-moving traffic and the occasional nut-job going ninety miles an hour, weaving perilously between lanes. But he made it. It seemed the entire city was one hill after another as he worked his way toward the Church of St. Agnes. When he hit the intersection of Haight and Ashbury, he immediately felt a sense of its history. The intersection and its neighborhood were the birthplace of the counterculture hippie movement in the sixties. He pictured Jim Morrison falling out of a car drunk or hippies in a circle smoking a pipe in a park. Willie was pretty young during the movement, but as a musician himself, he understood its significance.

He pulled across the street from Saint Agnes, crossed traffic, and tried the door. It was a weekday, and there was no Mass. He was a little shocked the door was open, so he went in. Captivated by the beauty of the sanctuary, Willie walked quietly down the main aisle to the third row, genuflected, and executed the sign of the cross, figuring, *when in Rome*. He sat in the pew and reached for the Bible in the rack in front of him. He found the Psalms and flipped to Psalm 33. There was nothing except a lot of words. Thinking it might be some sort of clue, he read the verse:

> *2 Praise the LORD with harp: sing unto him with the psaltery and an instrument of ten strings. 3 Sing unto him a new song; play skilfully with a loud noise.*

Willie laughed with a chuff. It seemed the thief had a sense of humor even when it came to something as sacred as the Bible, by including a reference to a stringed instrument.

He returned the book to its place, took the next one in line, and checked it. When he got to the page, a note and another picture of his guitar fell out. He opened the note, and it read:

I'm not telling you exactly where your guitar is because Mumm's the word. Champagne awaits you at the end of your quest. There you can get your guitar, get in your car, and just let it roll on down the highway.

Willie laughed at the reference to the song by Bachman Turner Overdrive. The song was certainly a favorite of his, with lyrics about life on the road as a rock and roller. He looked at the photo and, sure enough, his guitar was sitting next to the sign at the Mumm winery. His heart jumped a bit at the finality of the note. It seemed to indicate that his quest was almost done.

He took out his phone and Google-mapped the Mumm Winery. The results showed the location in Napa Valley, about an hour and twenty minutes away. Willie was ecstatic for a couple of reasons. He'd always thought it would be cool to see Napa Valley, as his ex-wife was a wine aficionado and had bugged him on numerous occasions about going there. More importantly, though, he knew he was close to having his guitar back—with any kind of luck.

Willie's jaw dropped as he approached the Golden Gate Bridge. The iconic structure and its amazing engineering he'd seen in so many television shows and movies was everything he'd expected and more. Despite the battleship-gray skies and cool, damp air, the bridge gave him a sense of life. It energized him. He was finally seeing the world, and it sparked his desire to see what lay beyond.

As the miles passed, Willie rocked out to his California Spotify playlist. He looked down at the USB charger dangling from his still-broken ignition. For some reason, it didn't bother him like it had when it first happened. In the grand scheme of things, based on the experiences he'd had in the past couple of days, it seemed insignificant. Those moments in Winslow and LA, then in San Francisco and

Napa, made the gravity of something like a broken possession seem smaller. He wasn't sure exactly where the change had happened, but it was definitely a change in thought. A change for the better.

Willie walked into the Mumm Winery and looked around. The smartly dressed female attendant on duty said, "Good afternoon, sir. May I help you?"

"Uh, yeah. I have a strange request. I'm looking for my guitar. Has anyone left one here?"

"Why yes, in fact, someone did. A couple of days ago. They instructed me to turn it over to you, given three conditions."

"That is fantastic news. What conditions?" Willie asked.

"First, I need an ID."

Willie pulled out his driver's license and showed it to the woman.

"You're a match," she said with a wink. "Next, I was told you need to purchase a bottle of our sparkling wine to celebrate your guitar recovery."

"No problem there. I'll take a bottle of your Brut Prestige," Willie said, pointing to the bottle on the shelf. He didn't care what kind he got as long as it led to his guitar and didn't require him to sell a kidney to afford it.

"A fine choice, sir. And finally, I'll need a key to open the case your guitar is in."

"Ah, yes! The key. I have it right here," he said, reaching into his pocket, pulling out his key ring, and showing it to her. He removed it from the ring and handed it over.

"Thank you. If you'll excuse me, I'll just be a minute. I need to go get it." She walked into the other room.

Willie stood there waiting in expectation, thinking to himself, *what a crazy trip.* A week ago, he was back home with nothing to look forward to except booking his next gig. Now, he was on the West Coast, buying champagne and seeing the country.

The woman returned with a brand-new guitar case in hand. She laid it on one of the standing tables and tried the key in the lock, and it clicked open. She undid the other buckles and opened the case. In it were an envelope and the Fender. Willie's eyes lit up at the sight of it. He pulled it out of the case and gave it a once-over. There was no visible damage that he could tell. It was exactly as he'd last seen it at the Blues Estate. It was a reunion worth every mile.

He tucked the envelope into his back pocket and thanked the woman. Willie put the guitar back in the case as she handed back the key. He tipped her twenty dollars for her trouble and walked out.

In his car, he opened the envelope and read the note.

Well, well, well. Your love of your guitar has taken you far! I hope it has instilled in you a love of travel. There's a big, beautiful world outside Milwaukee. Now go see it!
—A Friend

Willie lowered his hands and looked out the windshield. In front of him were rows and rows of grapevines warmed by a lovely California sun. It was positively breathtaking and made him realize the scene was exactly what her point was all along this journey. He knew the thief couldn't be anyone but his ex-wife, Jaime. Their split had been amicable, but he remembered her telling him he needed to grow, deal with his past, and realize what he had in the here and now. It was clear from the musical scavenger hunt he'd been on she was pushing him out of his comfort zone and getting him to expand his horizons.

Willie set the note on the passenger seat. He decided from that moment forward he'd call his precious guitar Jaime. She'd done way more for him in his life than Agatha ever did. Then he pulled out his phone, opened Google Maps, and typed Muir Woods, then Estes National Park, then Black Hills, then Paisley Park, and added them all to his route home. When he started the car, the John Hiatt song, "Adios to California," came on the Spotify stream. Willie smiled to himself and put the car in drive.

The Brethren of Postocrity

Levi Sampson didn't know what to make of the letter lying on his kitchen table. It arrived in the mail in a cream-colored business envelope with a New Orleans postmark. What jumped out immediately was CLASSIFIED! stamped on the front. When he flipped the envelope over, he was surprised to see it sealed with a circular wax seal featuring a pyramid with an infinity ribbon cutting through the center. There was no return address, which he thought was odd.

"Hmmm," he muttered to himself while breaking the seal and tearing the envelope open. The letter read:

Dear Mr. Sampson,

Unbeknownst to you, throughout your life, your actions have been monitored by the Brethren of Postocrity. The Brethren are a little-known forum of righteousness and justice composed of twelve gifted Postocrits. We and our forebears have been impacting world history for many centuries. While you are not privy to the details of all our gifts, talents, and magic, suffice it to say we do not take our influence lightly. Our current world is in a state of turmoil and struggle but trust me when I say it would be much worse if not for the actions of this forum.

So, after considerable deliberation and discussion, including a democratic vote, you have been granted two Profits of Temporal Shift by the Brethren of Postocrity. This is the most hallowed of privileges, given only to a few selected individuals periodically. Because of your history of sound moral choices and decisions, as well as your love for your fellow humans, the Brethren deem you a capable steward. However, they have also entrusted you to use these two coveted profits only in the pursuit of things righteous and good. Remember, you cannot change written history as we know it, but you may only alter what might have been for a single individual and those related to them.

Therefore, by reciting a specific date, time, and place at exactly 3:00 p.m. on your next two birthdays, you may return to the said date, time, and place. While there, you may partake in the events of that day; however, you cannot affect more than one historical variable. Whatever you do will have a profound effect on the life of someone, though may not change history for more than that person and any individuals immediately related to the event. After the change is effected, you will return to your current time and location. The Brethren assume you will invoke these profits with great care and an understanding of their impact.

With all due respect,
Fathom Richter, Grand Instigator
Brethren of Postocrity

Levi read the letter again, just to make sure he wasn't dreaming. What kind of witchcraft was this guy talking about, especially in suburban St. Paul, in 2015? Is this brethren organization even real, or some sort of scam? He opened Google on his phone and typed "Brethren of Postocrity." Only one hit came up. Levi couldn't recall ever having only one hit come up on Google for anything. It made the whole proposition all the more intriguing. The search result was an offer to sell him the internet domain name brethrenofpostocrity.com.

Levi had always been a closet dreamer and speculator. He believed there was a much bigger alien story, including a cover-up at Area 51. He was convinced the Loch Ness monster was real—some sort of amphibian, aquatic dinosaur. And to him, beasts like Yetis and Sasquatches were certainly within the realm of possibility. Maybe these brethren were aware of his tendency for the eccentric and improbable, and it might have played a part in his selection. He didn't have any answers, but the thought of doing a little time travel excited something within him. With his fifty-third birthday fast approaching in a week, he was giddy at the possibility of it all.

Levi tapped the keys on his laptop, googling events of historic significance. His imagination took him everywhere in place and time. He went all the way back to Paul Revere's ride on April 18, 1775. *What would it be like to have lived that long ago?* He wondered. While he kicked the idea around a bit, the thought of being stuck there, should something go wrong with the hocus pocus behind the time jump, left a lot to be desired. As bad as the world was today, he liked his modern conveniences, including indoor bathrooms, so 1775 seemed a bit too risky.

After a couple more dead-end searches, he ended up looking up the date of John F. Kennedy's assassination. He was two years old when it happened, so in the possibility that something glitched during the time jump, at least he would be left in a time period he'd lived in, even if it was in Texas. After some thought, he settled on the tragic event as the destination for the use of his first profit.

On the Saturday of Levi's birthday, he woke, got dressed, had breakfast, and went about his life. He did it knowing today was the day to determine if the whole "profit" thing was real.

Near the appointed hour, his nervousness ratcheted up. What was he getting into? Was it time to rethink the whole thing and back out? If he did, he might spend the rest of his life wondering what he'd potentially missed out on. If he went through with it and something glitched and he was left in 1963, what then? Life without the internet! Would his parents be young again, back in Wisconsin? If so, how would he find them, and would they freak out if he showed up as a fifty-three-year-old? Probably!

After struggling with the dilemma for some time, he stood in his living room at 2:59 p.m. As the clock struck 3:00 p.m., he said, "November 22, 1963, 12:28 p.m., Dealey Plaza in Dallas, Texas."

Levi was enveloped by cold air and after a second, he smelled what he thought was a mixture of sulfur and chlorine. He heard a sound like a passenger train and, in an instant, was standing at the doorway to the famous Book Depository building. The rectangular red-brick structure was immediately recognizable. He'd seen it in history books and various documentaries many times. Levi heard the buzz of a crowd from afar and, judging from the vintage of cars parked on the street, he was clearly in the right time period for what he'd come to do. He looked down at his clothes and was shocked to see he was wearing fashion right out of the sixties. A blue and white piped polo shirt, polyester flared pants, and Hush Puppy shoes.

He glanced at his watch. It showed 12:28 p.m. Realizing time was of the essence, he took off through the entrance of the building. He ran down a hallway, and when he found a door to the stairs, he opened it and sprinted up. By the fourth floor, his breathing was heavy, and he felt lightheaded. Still, he pressed on, bolting up the last two flights.

His heart was pounding when he finally reached the sixth floor. He exited the stairwell and ran to the room near the corner of the hallway. He heard a shot, then a second, as he opened the door slowly and silently. There in the corner, on one knee, was Lee Harvey Oswald. He fired a third shot out the window.

As Oswald reloaded, Levi heard him say, "And this one's for Jackie."

"Hey! What kind of coward shoots a woman?" Levi shouted.

Oswald turned around with a start. He jumped up with his gun and ran at Levi.

Again, Levi was enveloped in cold air and smelled sulfur and chlorine. He shut his eyes, and after a few seconds, opened them. He was surprised to find he was standing in his living room, where this whole situation started. His head spun at what had just transpired only a minute before. Was it a dream, or did he really just save Jackie Kennedy's life two minutes prior? It certainly seemed as real as anything he'd ever seen.

As his head cleared, he suddenly wished he'd been there a few seconds earlier, so he could have saved the President. Then, he recalled the letter mentioning his inability to affect or change history itself, but that of a related individual. He'd have to be satisfied with the thought he'd played a part in saving the life of Jackie. It was quite a birthday gift for a guy at fifty-three.

It had been a year since Levi had used his profit magic, and he was ready to do it again. Having a full year to think about choosing a date, place, and event to travel to was difficult for him. So was the idea that he might end up changing a person's life forever. It made his decision even more difficult. As he saw it, he just wanted to be part of history. He remembered the cars and buildings from his last time-jump to the sixties and how strange it felt to be present on that fateful day, not to mention the impact he'd had on Jackie's life thereafter. To experience a bit of the time and witness the particular event had almost been incentive enough.

With an increased sense of assurance that there would be no glitch this time, he once again positioned himself in his living room, prepared for the big moment. When the time came at three in the afternoon of his fifty-fourth birthday, he said, "April 10, 1912, 11:20 a.m. Southampton, England." With a rush of cold air and a sniff of sulfur and chlorine later, he was standing in a steward uniform on the gangplank of a monstrous luxury liner. Before him stood a short line of remaining passengers waiting to board. In his hand, he held a manifest that read, White Star Line - SS Titanic. The remaining passengers stood anxiously awaiting as the departure time was almost upon them. A sickly older gentleman, hunched over, cane in hand, handed Levi his passport. Levi checked it and verified the name and address against the manifest.

"Okay. Looks good, welcome aboard," he said.

Next in line stood a couple. The man was smartly dressed in a suit and wearing perfectly shined dress shoes. The woman he was with wore an elegant dress, pearls around her neck, and a fur coat. Levi couldn't help but notice the smell of her expensive cologne.

"Passport and tickets, please," Levi asked.

The gentleman thrust the paperwork toward Levi. They were both haughty and dismissive in their manner toward him, as though his role as a steward made him lower class. The gentleman spoke up. "I can't believe they make us stand in the same line as everyone else. I paid good money for this passage and besides, don't they know I'm a Blake?" He appeared to be put off by the validation process, like it was an inconvenience they should not be troubled with.

Levi barely glanced at the passport and manifest and said, "Enjoy your journey, Mr. and Mrs. Blake."

Without a word of thanks or acknowledgment, they took their passports and walked up the gangplank arm-in-arm in a huff.

Levi stared into the tired eyes of the next passenger for a moment. She was a beautiful woman carrying her swaddled newborn in one arm and a bag in the other. She appeared laden with all the weariness that comes with young motherhood. He hesitated momentarily and said, "Passport and ticket, please."

She passed him her documents. He scanned them over and feigned a cross-check with the manifest.

"I'm sorry, madam, but it appears there's an error with your documents. Your name does not appear on the ship's manifest. You'll have to report back to the customs office. They can check your records or call the central office in London to verify your travel status," Levi said.

"What? There must be some mistake! My daughter and I have to get to New York, and the bloody ship is set to sail any minute. I'll never make it."

"I'm sorry, madam, but rules are rules. The office is just a short ten-minute walk up the road from here, but you'll have to hurry," Levi said.

She glanced at his name badge and said, "My word, you are not helpful! Fine. If my daughter and I miss this journey, I will hold you personally responsible. You are jeopardizing our future in America. I hope you can live with yourself, Mr. Sampson."

The woman turned and stomped furiously away in the direction of the customs office. The Titanic's whistle signaled its final blast before departure.

Cool air enveloped Levi.

Just What I Thought

Tony was always a keep-to-himself kind of guy. He'd taken enough personality tests to know he was an introvert and a follower, certainly not one to lead the pack. Tall, with dark hair and green eyes, he carried himself with a fake level of self-confidence in the hope no one would call his bluff and see him for the socially insecure person he was. He knew his place and didn't rock the boat in social situations because he just wanted people to like him. He knew his need for acceptance was a character shortcoming, but he couldn't really change who he was. Some things are just part of one's DNA or are learned behaviors that stick, for better or worse.

After getting a bachelor's degree in political science, he took a job at FastTech Industries, an application development company based in Phoenix. He was assigned to the Midwest branch in St. Paul, on the edge of downtown. Even though it wasn't related to what he went to school for, he liked the variety, and his co-workers were cool thirty-somethings, most with a tenure of less than five years. It was a fun staff, and he had a good relationship with everyone except Marissa Kenilworth, a fellow developer. She gave off a distinct vibe of disliking Tony.

He wasn't sure why Marissa was so cold and aloof, and wished he could read her mind. Tony tried to think of what he'd said to her over the couple of years they'd worked together that made him the enemy. At one point he'd caught a security flaw in one of her apps as part of the peer review software QC, but wasn't that what peer reviews were for? He'd brought it to light at the weekly staff meeting, not intending to smear her, but she might have perceived it as an attack. "Nice catch. I'll look into fixing that," she had replied. Judging from her body language, Tony sensed she hadn't appreciated the timing of his critique. He regretted it immediately, but the damage had already been inflicted. There was no taking the words back.

After work on a Tuesday, Tony slipped on his sneakers and headed for home. His commute was a mile and a half, and parking was such a hassle, it was just easier to walk to work. He got to his apartment a little after five o'clock and greeted his cat, Nandor, who met him at the door every day. "Hey, buddy. How's Nandor today?" Nandor curved around Tony's legs with quiet meows and an obvious need for affection. Tony reached and scratched the cat's neck for a moment, then headed to the kitchen to start dinner.

Tony turned on the old electric stove to preheat for his dinner. Another frozen pizza. He knew it was a culinary cop-out, but he didn't have it in him to fix anything else. Five minutes later he returned to the kitchen and while bracing himself with one hand on the metal overhead hood, he grabbed the oven door handle when Pfzzzzittt! Tony's vision went blindingly white for a moment as he was jolted backward by an electrical shock that coursed through his arms and torso.

"Yeow! What the fuck?" he said, literally shocked by what had just happened. He shook his head.

He knew the stove was old and realized he'd created a closed circuit by touching the two metal surfaces simultaneously. This would warrant a call to the landlord to have it fixed. It was clear something wasn't grounded correctly.

Tony grabbed a potholder and, being careful not to touch anything else, opened the oven door and slid his pizza in. He was hungry enough to risk another shock but was glad when nothing happened. When it was done, he ate it in front of the television. After an hour of mindlessness, his head throbbed with signs of an oncoming headache. He rarely suffered from them but figured perhaps something from the whole shock incident had triggered it. As the night went on, it worsened to where he saw an early bedtime as a remedy for a situation that wasn't improving.

Tony walked into the office the next day feeling much better. His headache had passed overnight, and he felt at the top of his game again. It was a crisp late-summer morning with hints of the shorter, cooler fall days ahead.

"Good morning, Tina," he said to the receptionist.

"Morning, Tony," she replied. *God, who dressed you this morning? Black pants and a blue shirt? Dude!*

Tony wrinkled his brow and turned back toward Tina. "I'm sorry, what?"

"I didn't say anything," Tina said with a smile.

"Oh, okay. I really should get my hearing checked," he replied awkwardly.

Tina smiled and turned back to her computer. As Tony walked, he heard another whisper in his head, *Whoa, that was weird. I wonder if my face gave away his fashion emergency.*

He shook his head to clear it. He smiled at the crazy thought he was suddenly hearing Tina's voice and thoughts. Stuff like that only happened in the movies. He figured he must be making them up in his head. Earlier that year, his personality profile inventory at work had defined him as a "Highly Sensitive Person," or HSP. One manifestation of this was words and actions affected him in ways not found in others. Maybe this voice was just some form of that.

He continued back through the maze of cubicles to his workstation. As he passed each one, he said hi to his coworkers. "Hi, Liz."

"Hi Tony." *Five minutes late again, I see.*

"Morning, Zach."

"Mornin' dude." *Oh my God, every morning he says hi. Every fricken morning!*

Tony cocked his head confusedly and continued. "Good morning, Ben."

"Morning, Tony," *Got that thirty dollars you owe me yet, or do I have to beg for it?*

As Tony walked, he wondered what was going on. *Am I the only one who can hear what these people are thinking? Furthermore, I thought I had paid Ben back already.*

Tony continued to his desk and booted up his computer. His cubicle was centered against Sonya on one side and Javier on the other. As he sat, he listened carefully to see if he could hear their thoughts. Nothing but silence. Tony took some reassurance from that. He began to think what he'd heard in his previous encounters was just a fluke.

Tony's supervisor, Perry, leaned into his cube and said, "Hey Tony, don't forget to fill out your timesheet today." *It's sort of pathetic I have to remind you of this every week, but hey, job security for me, I guess.*

"No problem. I appreciate the reminder," he replied. Evidently, his forgetfulness about the blasted timesheets must be a bone of contention with his boss. If he weren't so overworked on various projects, he'd certainly have more time to fill out his stinking timesheet.

That he could hear Perry's thoughts was disconcerting, though. Turns out all those thoughts he'd heard along on his way to his desk were real after all. Only people he made eye contact with were the ones whose thoughts could be heard. As long as he never looked at anyone for the rest of his life, there would be no problem. Seemed easy enough. He laughed and shook his head and began checking his emails.

Tony's cell phone trilled. He picked it up, saw it was his friend Chris, and answered.

"Hey buddy, Chris. Do you want to go to O'Gara's tonight? It's two-for-one until nine and, more importantly, it's ladies' night."

Tony's best friend had a persuasive way of convincing him to go out and spend money at the bars instead of saving it. After the strange day Tony had at work, he thought it might be a good diversion from his newly discovered superpower. He aimed to see if it was just a work thing or if it was going to bleed into his social life as well.

"Sure thing, Chris. That sounds good. I'll pick you up at eight if that's okay?"

"Cool. That's perfect. See you then," Chris said.

As he hung up the phone, it occurred to him he had heard nothing except what Chris was actually saying. Maybe Chris was just not thinking about anything other than the pending outing with Tony. Or it could have been as he had initially thought; perhaps it was because he never established eye contact with him. It's possible that it was a phenomenon influenced by social proximity. It was too early to tell. He was looking forward to seeing what happened at the bar, though. It could certainly play an interesting role in his romantic pursuits.

It was eighties retro night at O'Gara's. When they walked in, the speakers were thumping Peter Gabriel's song, "Sledgehammer," as bartenders hustled drinks from one patron to the next. It was a young crowd and busy but not packed. As they weaved through toward the bar, Tony picked up on thoughts from a few of the women.

He caught the eye of a short, attractive brunette nursing a vodka and cranberry. Instantly he heard, *Another one too tall. Damnit!* He wasn't sure what that was all about. He was 6'4" but guessed height mattered more to women than men. In any case, it ruled out any desire he might have had to pursue the woman.

Further on, a blonde sitting in a booth to his right momentarily locked eyes with him, and he heard, *In your dreams, big guy. Keep moving. God, I hate this dating scene. I just want to go home and binge some Netflix.*

"Wow," he said aloud.

"What? This crowd?" Chris asked.

"Uh, no. I'll tell ya later," he said, waving him off.

Moving through the crowd, he spotted Marissa from work talking to a friend over a drink. She looked at him, and her thought came immediately. *Ugh, Tony. What an arrogant asshole. Calling me out in a meeting. Nice, you jerk.*

Tony thought, well, I guess that answers my question about why she hates me. After the initial eye contact, Marissa glanced away, and he lost her train of thought.

Chris spotted a couple leaving one of the booths and made a beeline for it. The two friends slid in and claimed it.

"You want a beer? I'll get the first round," Tony asked.

"Sure, get me an IPA," Chris answered.

Tony worked his way up to the bar and situated himself to get the bartender's attention. Two stools down, he caught the eye of an attractive brunette gazing his way. She was slender, with a black and white waist-length sweater, yoga pants, and flats. Long, elegant earrings hung from her ears as she flicked her hair flirtatiously. He met her gaze for a full five seconds. During it, he again ascertained her thoughts. *Oh my God, look at his eyes. And that build! Take me home!*

Tony turned and realized the bartender was waiting to take his order.

"Oh, sorry, can I get two Hop Cone IPAs, please?"

As the bartender turned away, Tony turned back to the woman, who was again gazing at him. *I hope he gets the hint and comes over. If he does, he better not be a creep like that last jerk. That freak had octopus arms on the first date. What a mauler. C'mon dude, talk to me! I wonder if…*

As she turned away to talk to her girlfriend, he stopped gleaning what she was thinking. It left him hanging as to what she was wondering before she turned away. His mind spun with the possibilities. Does she wonder if I'm available? Or if I'm a good kisser? Or she might be wondering if Chris would hit it off with her girlfriend. He realized his mind was asking many of the same questions as it did before he could read thoughts. The difference, of course, was that he now knew what others were thinking ahead of him, so he had the upper hand.

"Here ya go," he said, handing Chris his beer. "Hey, that woman dressed in black and white is giving me the eye." Tony nodded toward the brunette woman just as she caught his gaze again. *Hey, you. Come on over. Gosh, this drink is weak. I wish Sarah would stop talking about her damn dog. She worships that stupid thing.*

Chris craned his neck around slowly to see who Tony was talking about. "Hey, she's pretty hot, and her friend's not bad either."

"You want to go over and introduce ourselves? I have a good feeling about this one," Tony said.

"How can you tell? We just got here." *What's with Tony tonight? He's on the make. I don't want to be left alone if he gets lucky.*

"I don't know. Call it intuition, but she's too hot not to at least say hi," Tony replied after taking a sip of his beer.

"I've never seen you move quite this fast before, but okay." Chris glanced at the girls again to see if they were worth all the hype. They were both looking at Tony and him.

We're losing a great seat in this booth. This better work.

"It will, don't worry," Tony said.

"Wait, what? Are you a mind-reader or something?"

"What are you talking about?" Tony replied.

"It's like you just answered what I was thinking in my head."

"I don't know what you mean. Let's go meet these ladies."

They grabbed their beers and walked over to the two women. On the way, Tony heard, *Oh my God, he's coming over and bringing his friend! I wonder if my hair is okay. Play it cool. God, he's gorgeous. Don't say anything stupid. Be aloof, yet approachable.*

Tony thought, *Wow, do all women think this much?* "Hi, you ladies both look familiar. Do we know you?" Tony asked.

The brunette woman flicked her hair and giggled, "Um, I don't think so." *This guy's smooth. That's a good opening line.*

"Thanks, it's one of my favorite openers," Tony said.

The ladies looked at him quizzically.

He realized he'd answered her thought. He quickly regrouped to cover his gaffe. "Uh, I mean, I thought you seemed familiar. My name's Tony, and this is Chris. And you are..."

"I'm Kate, and this is Charlene."

"Those names ring a bell for you, Chris?"

"Uh, nope. But nice to meet you both, nonetheless."

The conversation ebbed and flowed as the evening progressed. Tony had a difficult time filtering the many thoughts from three people at once but was fortunate to have the voices change in pitch by person, so he could separate the important thoughts from the mundane. From what he was hearing, Chris was trying to get Charlene to look his way, but after a few tries, he'd concluded she was stuck up. From Charlene, he heard she was obsessed with an accounting error she'd made at work and also sorely missed her dog, Peanuts. She'd also repeated more than once how she hated being a part of Kate's sexual pursuits.

Tony got the inside edge on Kate from the many thoughts she sent his way. It was almost criminal how he could use them to steer the conversation to his advantage. It was clearly benefiting him as Kate gave him visual cues, like touching his arm occasionally to make a point. At the same time, Charlene and Chris were not getting along as Tony had hoped. Charlene kept gazing off into the distance as if she were searching for someone. At 11:30, Tony looked at Kate and got the thought he'd hoped for all along.

Ugh, I'm tired and want to go home. I hope this guy asks for my number before we leave.

"Well, it's getting late, and I have work in the morning. Chris and I should be going. This has been fun. We should hang out again."

Yes, we should…at least you and I should! "It has been fun. That sounds cool." Kate said.

Pulling out his phone, Tony said, "Why don't you give me your number, and I'll call you sometime?"

Oh, this is perfect. Kate recited her number, and Tony typed it into his phone. Charlene was not forthcoming with hers, and it became clear she and Chris were not interested in pursuing things beyond this bar. The couples walked to the door and parted ways.

"Well, that went well…for you," Chris said.

"Yeah, it didn't seem like you and Charlene were hitting it off."

"I don't know. She just seemed sort of stuck-up to me."

"Yeah, I gleaned that."

"There you go again, claiming to read my mind. And not too far from actually doing it, I might add."

"What? Uh, yeah, do you want to get some food? I have something I want to talk about," Tony asked.

"Sure, let's go to Mama Rochelle's."

Tony picked at his strawberry crepes while Chris dug into his omelet.

"So what's up, man? What's on your mind?" Chris said, taking a bite of his food. *This needs salt!*

Tony handed the saltshaker to Chris unannounced. Chris looked at him and locked his gaze. *What the fuck is going on?*

"I'll tell you what the fuck's going on. I can hear your thoughts. And now that you know my secret, I think you should apologize to Charlene for what you were fantasizing about at the bar."

Chris blushed beet red for a moment, knowing he'd had sexual thoughts about getting Charlene to sleep with him.

"Wait. Are you kidding me? Read my thoughts? What the actual fuck? When did you gain this superpower, or whatever it is?"

"That's why we're here. I started hearing thoughts today as I went into work. I don't know how it happened, but it did. As far as I can tell, it's not everyone's thoughts, only those who catch my gaze or to whom I am talking. It doesn't seem to work over the phone, thank goodness. That's all I need."

The things I would do if I had this! Money, women, swindling…

"I will be doing none of that, by the way. Well, maybe the women thing for a while," Tony said with a laugh.

"For cripe's sake, I've got to stop thinking about stuff when I'm around you. This is creepy as fuck; you realize that, don't you?"

"I do. But I'm not sure what to do about it yet."

"Maybe start by seeing a doctor, or, better yet, a psychiatrist," Chris suggested.

Tony laughed. That was his first thought, but he was thinking it might be a good social experiment to read a few of the people in his life and see what they were really made of. See if they were what they advertised.

"Okay, well, maybe I will. But I want to see where it takes me these next couple of days. It's been weirdly insightful, and I'm not sure I'm ready to give it up just yet."

"Well, that's great to hear, but it means I can't hang around you. You know that, right? I don't need someone snooping around my head when I least expect it. It's an invasion of privacy, if nothing else. Dude, this is the weirdest, most powerful affliction I've ever heard of."

Tony knew and had thought the same thing himself. But his life had also become predictable and mundane, so this new gift—if that's what you would call it—was a welcome diversion from the routine.

Tony took a sip of his coffee and nodded. "I know, I know. But do me a favor and don't tell anyone just yet. And then, check back with me by phone periodically through the week, and I'll let you know how it's going. Remember, I can't read your thoughts unless I can see your eyes."

"Well, I sure as hell won't be FaceTiming you anytime soon, you can be sure of that."

"Ha! You know, none of this would be a problem if people had clean thoughts and pure motives. It's a reminder to reflect and consider what you think about—is what I'm trying to say. If some people's minds weren't so twisted, we'd all be better off," Tony said.

"Yeah, well, our thoughts are also where we work out everything before we put it into action. Thankfully, we don't all do or say what we think. That's what makes us human and, more importantly, civilized. Monkeys think, *'I'm going to throw poo,'* and then they throw poo. Humans work that shit out in their heads and then act like decent people—no pun intended."

Tony had to admit, Chris had a good point.

The walk to work the following Monday was business as usual, back to another work week. As he came to the area near the bridge over the Mississippi River, he saw a homeless guy sitting on a bench. He sported a long beard, and his winter coat was dirty and worn. Before Tony could even look away, as he often did during encounters with the homeless, he heard,

This guy will pass, pretending he doesn't see me. God, I'm hungry. I'd kill for a breakfast sandwich at McDonald's.

The voice in his head caused Tony to start. What right did that guy have to judge him without cause? Granted, the guy was right; Tony did plan to pass him, feigning blindness to his presence, but still.

As he neared the man, he switched his path and headed toward him. The man watched him with sad hope in his eyes. Tony drew out his wallet and pulled out a twenty.

"Good morning, sir. How are you doing today?" Tony asked.

"Hello. I'm okay. It's the best I can do today, I guess."

"That it is, sir. I wanted to give this to you. Get yourself a breakfast sandwich at McDonald's or something."

He watched as the man's eyes widened. Tony wasn't sure if the look was directed at Tony's apparent ability to read his mind or the denomination of the bill he was handed. He looked at the bill and back up at Tony. "Well, thank you kindly. I was just thinking about that very thing. God bless you, son."

Oh my goodness, thank God for this guy. I'm getting two McMuffins and a coffee today! "No worries. What's your name?"

"Phillip."

"Well, you have a great day, Phillip, and take care." Tony walked away with a momentary feeling of gratitude for the gift he'd been granted. His ability to listen into the mind of this soul, this person, this fellow human, had pushed him outside the confines of his normally selfish behavior. He thought to himself, if nothing else positive happens today, it's already been a good day.

Despite his brief interaction with Phillip, Tony arrived at the office fifteen minutes early. He'd remembered what Liz had thought about his tardiness last week, and he aimed to correct it. When he walked in, he saw Tina at the reception desk. "Hey, Tina. Looking good today. I love the color of that blouse. Very flattering."

Tina blushed a little after her initial surprise and responded coyly, "Why, thank you, Tony. You're looking sharp yourself today." *And no blue and black combo either. There might still be hope for him yet.*

"Thanks. I think there might still be hope for my fashion sense," he replied. Tony watched her eyebrows raise and kept walking. His thought-reading was proving to be great fun at times.

As he passed Liz's desk, he made it a point to look at his watch after he said, "Good morning, Liz."

"Morning, Tony. . ." *Wow, quarter to eight. This is unprecedented.* "My, you're here early."

"Yeah, I'm trying to work on my punctuality. Making some changes in my life."

Well, it's about time.

"I figure it's about time," Tony said and moved along, noticing Liz's surprise. He spotted Zach in his cubicle. He'd remembered Zach's annoyance with Tony's daily greeting, so walked by silently.

Zach caught his eye as he passed, and Tony heard, *Wow. Okay, that was weird. No hello today? Wonder if something's up with Tony?*

Tony thought it was best to keep Zach guessing, so he kept moving. Again, he marveled at how advantageously fun this skill could be. The last desk he had to traverse on his way to his cubicle was Ben's. "Good morning, Ben. Hey, here's that thirty bucks I owe you. Sorry it's so late. I was waiting until today's payday."

"Oh, thanks, man. I'd completely forgotten about it. Appreciate it," Ben replied, taking the money from Tony. *What, no interest? I guess I should just be happy I got it back at all.*

Tony took a step toward his own office, then stopped and spun on his heel. He reached into his wallet and pulled out a bill. "And hey, here's an extra five for being so patient," Tony said.

"Wow, you don't have to do that. I didn't expect interest."

"No, no, I insist. It helped me out of a jam, and I appreciate it."

Sweet! Maybe Tony's not a schmuck after all.

"No problem. I know I hate it when people don't pay me back. The schmucks!" Tony replied. Out of the corner of his eye, he saw Ben's eyebrows raise as he turned and walked toward his cubicle. Tony grinned broadly, sat down, and powered up his computer.

Tony spent Sunday night getting into his pre-Monday routine. Tonight was Shake n' Bake chicken night, pushing the full extent of his culinary expertise. He usually cooked half a chicken and used the leftovers for lunch the next day. Canned corn and a side of bread rounded out his bachelor meal.

He leaned over to open the oven and braced himself by grabbing the top of the stove while holding the door handle. Pfzzzitt! Again, he felt an electric jolt and was blinded by a momentary flash of white light.

"Holy fuck!" he cursed himself for forgetting about the stupid stove. He needed to call the landlord and get it checked. The next shock might be his last.

Tony walked into work on Monday, backpack slung over his shoulder, ready to take on the onslaught of thoughts that would come his way.

"Good morning, Tina."

"Morning, Tony," she replied.

Tony hesitated momentarily, waiting for her thought to come into his head. Nothing. Hmmm, was it possible she just wasn't thinking anything at the time? He guessed it was. It was just weird he hadn't encountered it before now.

He walked past Liz's desk. "What's up, Liz?"

"Nothing much, Tony. Good morning."

Again, he hesitated, this time stopping altogether. Again, there was no thought.

"What's wrong?" Liz asked.

"What? Oh, nothing. Just trying to remember if I brought my thermos of coffee with me this morning," he replied, trying to cover his tracks.

He proceeded to his desk and never heard another voice in his head the rest of the day. When he got home, he spent the night ruminating. He wasn't sure how he felt about the loss of a situationally useful skill, nor how it had happened. What triggered it? What had he done since Saturday that might have negated the power?

The answer hit him like the shock from the night before. *The stove! Of course!* The timing of both shocks coincided with the gain and subsequent loss of the thought-reading. It suddenly made sense.

He realized he'd learned so much about himself and the human nature of so many others during his brief time of giftedness. He'd seen the nastiness people held in their minds, including his own. His intentions with Kate from the bar were a perfect example. Having an edge on the thoughts of a woman could work to his advantage, especially regarding working the dating scene. It did, however, take away a bit of the mystique between men and women. He had to admit he liked that part of dating life.

And then there was what he'd learned about people's perceptions of him. That was incredibly enlightening. It gave him insight into some of his annoying behavior. After assessing them, he made some changes in his life. He felt he was a better person after changing some things to improve himself as a friend and coworker. He concluded he enjoyed being able to read people's thoughts and wasn't sure he was ready to part with it.

What are the chances I could get the skill back? One in a million, probably. A total fluke.

Tony turned on the oven and stood in front of it for a few minutes, deliberating. Then he reached for the vent and the door handle.

A Cast of 10,000

The light rain fell softly, like one of those sappy rock ballads from the early eighties. The morning had started overcast on the Turtle Flambeau Flowage, but an annoying drizzle became part of the annual muskie outing for Jeremy and his friends. He and Steve were city boys who loved to fish, and this fall muskie trip had become a fun tradition. They were fortunate to have their friend Tom host them at his cabin and take them fishing in his seventeen-foot Crestliner.

Tom guided the boat around the lake using his trolling motor remote control. He worked the boat with deftness and certainty. "Remember, boys, what are the three most important elements in muskie fishing?" Tom asked.

"Boat control. Fucking boat control. And, goddamn boat control," Jeremy replied.

"Exactly," Tom confirmed.

Out the back of the boat, two large bobbers floated on the surface, one to the port side, one starboard. While Tom monitored the bobbers and the trolling motor, Jeremy and Steve cast lures the size of small lap dogs toward the shore. This strategy of two to four baits in the water maximized the chances of landing a muskie. They usually landed at least one fish a year. Muskies are notoriously hard to catch, rightfully earning them the title: the fish of 10,000 casts.

Steve and Tom talked about the problems with the Wisconsin Badgers' running game. In the bow, Jeremy was in the trance known as "inattentive casting." When you sling lures for seven hours without seeing a fish, you almost fall into a hypnotic trance. In the middle of it, he felt a fish slam the lure. It caught him by surprise, and instinctively he reared back and set the hook like a champ. The fish turned and dove momentarily, exposing its side. Jeremy saw a flash of deep green in the water as he struggled to control the rod and reel it in.

"Fish on! Oh, it's a good one too," Jeremy shouted. Steve reeled in his lure while Tom snapped to work, getting the big net ready. Jeremy's fish thrashed and fought with vengeance and attitude. As it neared the boat, it got spooked and again dove toward the bottom.

"Put your rod in the water, rod in the water," Tom coached. This was a way to ensure the fish wouldn't snap the line either by brute force or on a rivet on the underside of the boat. Jeremy followed Tom's lead and plunged the top half of the rod into the water to give the fish room to move and tire. As it relented, Jeremy pulled the rod up and reeled in the slack. The fish made a last-ditch attempt to throw the hook with a death roll, but Tom dipped the net deep and got underneath the muskie and bagged it.

"Yeah! Got her!" Jeremy yelled.

"Yes, we did. Nice work!" Tom added.

The three exchanged high fives. Tom grabbed the release tools and set to work, freeing the treble hooks from the fish's mouth. His years of muskie fishing had made him an expert at reaching the hooks and freeing the fish, so Steve and Jeremy looked on as he worked.

"It looks like a forty-five incher or so, from what I can see down here," Tom said.

After Tom freed the muskie, he grabbed it by the gill and lifted it into the boat. As he slid his hand under its belly and turned to hand the fish to Jeremy for a picture, he felt a jolt of electricity course through his body. "Yeow!" Tom screamed as he stiffened, shuddered, and dropped the fish on the floor of the boat where it flipped and flopped maniacally.

"Dude, what the fuck, man? Did she cut you or something? I'll get her," Jeremy said, bending down to pick up the fish. Before Tom had a chance to answer, Jeremy picked up the muskie. As he straightened up, he looked like he'd stuck a butter knife in an electrical socket. His eyes bugged out, and he shivered and shook. He shook his hands as if they'd been scorched.

"Holy shit!" he said, dropping the fish much like Tom had. Again, the fish flopped in shock, trying to find its way back to the lake. "What the actual fuck? That fish just gave me 10,000 volts!"

"I was going to tell you that, but you beat me to it by picking it up," Tom said with a self-righteous laugh.

"Guys, what the hell? It's only a muskie for cripe's sake," Steve said, making his way toward the flopping fish.

"I wouldn't touch that fucker if I were you. Or, if you do, you might want to ground yourself on something," Tom warned.

"Really? It's not like it's an electric eel or anything," Steve said. He bent down to pick up the slimy fish currently fighting for air. As he got ready to tuck his fingers behind the gill, he hesitated momentarily. Before he lost his courage, he grabbed the fish by the gill and the tail. When he stood up, he was pushed backward as if kicked by a mule. He fell to the floor of the boat and smashed his back against the gunwale.

"Ow! What the actual fuck is with that thing?" he said.

Tom and Jeremy laughed at their friend writhing in pain.

"I told you so, man. It's some sort of electro-Frankenstein fish or something," Jeremy said.

The fish continued to flop as the three friends looked at one another in befuddlement.

"Well, at this stage, I'd say a picture of you holding it is out of the question," Tom said to Jeremy with a laugh.

"Aw man, that sucks. It's a beautiful fish, and it put up a great fight. I'll get a shot of her on the floor here." Jeremy pulled out his phone and snapped a couple of pictures after the fish had momentarily settled. The fish was long and thick through the middle. As Tom had predicted, it had to be in the low forties for length.

"As evil as this fish is, we should get her back in the water. How are we going to do that without getting jolted?" Tom asked.

"Maybe we could scoop her with the net and drop it in that way," Jeremy suggested.

"Good idea," Steve said, grabbing the net from the back of the boat. He slid it under the fish, and the muskie jerked. A bolt of energy lit the entire length of the net handle. Steve's hands clamped onto the net as he held it, shuddering as he was helpless to let go.

"Let go, man! Let go!" Tom shouted.

Steve shook as if he were having an epileptic seizure. All he could muster was "Cccccaaannnn'ttt…"

Tom went over and kicked the fish off of the metal edge of the net. Steve dropped the handle, stopped shaking, and slumped in a heap on the bottom of the boat. His eyes rolled in their sockets for a few seconds before he snapped out of it.

"Man… What the fuck was that?" Steve asked.

"Ya got jolted a good one. You okay?" Jeremy asked.

"I think so. My ears are burning, and my fingertips are a little numb, but I think I'm okay." Steve got back to his feet and stood looking at the fish with the other guys. The fish lay there, aspirating, its gills heaving breaths of cold northern air.

Jeremy pointed at the muskie and said, "Look at that thing. It's laughing at us."

True to his point, it seemed to be wearing a grin on its long, green snout. Its eyes rolled from person to person, almost as if it was making sure they saw it. The three guys looked at one another and laughed. They'd been shocked and punked by a muskie, and now it appeared to be mocking them.

"So, what are we going to do with this fish, man? It's sparking people up like a bad jump with a car battery," Jeremy said.

"I wonder why I didn't get shocked while pulling it out of the net?" Tom asked.

"Maybe it's got something to do with closing the circuit. You might have closed it by touching it with two hands, or something," Jeremy offered.

"Yeah, and Steve was holding the net with both hands," Tom added.

Tom looked at Jeremy and said, "You grab the tail, and I'll grab it under the gill, and we'll see if we can heave it overboard."

The two of them surrounded the fish. "We'll count to three, grab it, and throw it over this side," Jeremy said, pointing to the starboard side of the boat. Jeremy hitched up his pants and crouched down to grab the tail.

Tom counted, "One, two…" When he said three, the fish started flopping with new aggressiveness. It angled and arched its long body and lifted high into the air, reaching eye level with many of its thrashing jumps. Jeremy caught a tail slap on his cheek during one of the more impressive leaps. The fish didn't appear fatigued at all. The shocks it had delivered seemed to energize it.

"What the fuck? The thing's possessed," Steve said, now cowering in the boat's bow. The fish continued flopping in the middle of the boat as the guys scattered to the fringes.

"How are we going to get this thing back in the water without electrocuting ourselves?" Jeremy asked.

"That's the $10,000 question, genius," Tom answered.

Jeremy said, "We could just let it flop until it dies, but I hate killing any muskie, even the zombie-electrified ones."

"Well, frankly, I'd like to get some more fishing in before we call it a day, so let's figure out a plan here," Steve said.

The fish continued to flop mercilessly, sometimes even head high, from one end of the boat to the other. "Hey, Jeremy, hand me that oar," Tom said.

Jeremy grabbed the oar from the bottom of the boat and handed it to him. Tom took it and said, "Here's what I'm gonna do. When this fucker flips high enough, I'm going to turn him into a line shot down the baseline, so you guys might wanna cover up and stay low. Wood doesn't conduct electricity, so I think this will work."

Steve and Jeremy took seats in the bow and stern, respectively. Tom gripped the oar at the midpoint of its shaft and held it like a baseball bat. The muskie continued flopping low to the boat as Tom waited for the right pitch, as it were. At the moment, everything was low and inside. He wanted it in the strike zone.

"Try not to hurt the thing too badly, man. I mean, you only need to swing for a single, not a home run," Jeremy said.

"Thanks, Captain Obvious. You're such a compassionate fucker. I'll hit it enough that it will always remember me. Besides, the thing jolted me. It needs a little shock of its own from me."

The fish started back into its high-flopping fit, and Tom swung the oar and hit it right in the midsection. Slime flew in all directions as the fish bowed into a U shape from the force. It sailed about three feet from the boat and splashed ungracefully into the water. A small puff of smoke rose from the surface where it entered.

"And Tom hits a liner in the gap for a single!" Steve exclaimed.

Jeremy laughed and said, "What the fuck? Was that smoke?"

"It sure was. It's not surprising, given everything else about this fish," Tom added.

Tom sat between the other two guys at the Muskie Fin bar drinking beers and nibbling at deep-fried cheese curds and spicy chicken wings. Ben the bartender poured a bucket of ice into the sink behind the bar, getting ready for the evening crowd. ESPN played NFL highlights on the big-screen TVs sprinkled around the bar. A couple of slot machines sat in the corner begging for attention with bright lights and false promises of financial gain. Three other locals were across the bar nursing Miller Lites and waiting for a conversation to come their way.

"Ben, you're not going to believe what happened to us today," Tom said.

Ben set the bucket underneath the bar and said, "What's that?"

"So, we catch this beautiful muskie, and when I pick it up out of the net, I get an electric shock, just like I'd put a knife in a socket or something."

"What? For real?"

"Dude, I cannot make this shit up. All three of us were shocked by the thing at some point. Plus, the thing flopped like it was possessed." Steve and Jeremy nodded their agreement.

"Wow, that's freaky," Ben said.

One of the locals wearing a Stormy Kromer cap near the end of the bar spoke up and said, "Did you say the fish shocked you?"

"Yes, sir, all three of us. Why? Do you know something we don't?" Tom asked.

"Well, they had a big accident at the hydro plant in Park Falls last week. There was some sort of surge event that resulted in a big fish kill in the area. I wonder if this is related?"

"Does that river feed into the Turtle Flambeau Flowage in Mercer?" Steve asked.

"Sure does. It would mean the fish had to swim upstream, but they move around anyway," the Stormy Kromer guy said.

"That's creepy as hell, actually," Steve said. He pulled out his phone and opened the photo gallery. He thumbed through the images, but all he found were pictures of the bottom of the boat. None had the fish in them.

"What the…? Hey, did either of you get a picture of the fish?" Steve asked.

"I figured you two were taking them, so I didn't bother," Tom said.

"Hold on," Jeremy said, pulling his phone out of his pocket and scrolling through the pictures. He scrolled back and forth a few times before saying, "Evidently, I don't have any pictures, either. Just the bottom of Tom's boat. Dang, I know I took at least one photo of the fish."

The Stormy-Kromer-cap guy sat there grinning, then piped up. "So let me get this straight. You caught an electric muskie that is camera shy? Bahahaha!" The other two locals cracked up and backslapped Stormy. Even Ben smiled broadly at the snide joke.

Ben spoke up and said, "Evidently they're the fish of every 10,000th picture, too!"

The three locals howled with laughter again.

"Hey, man, we aren't lying. This shit happened. I don't know how to explain the pictures, but it all happened," Jeremy said defensively.

"No, I ain't saying it didn't happen. It just might have been more believable had there been some photographic evidence. Kinda like them Hodags!" Stormy said with a laugh. His reference was to the terrifying but mythical horned creature that was legendary in the area. It drew more laughter from his beer-drinking cronies.

"Yeah, well, it is what it is, man. Whatever," Tom said and looked away dismissively. The conversations split back up, as each of the groups lowered their voices to keep it to themselves. As they talked quietly, the jukebox taunted the fishermen as it played Joe Walsh's song, "Life of Illusion." As appropriate as it was to the situation, it certainly wasn't helping matters any.

Tom turned to Steve and said, "Drink up, man. We're getting out of here. We're becoming laughingstocks." Then he leaned over and whispered the same thing to Jeremy. The three of them slugged back the tail end of their beers and set their glasses on the bar. Tom threw a fiver on the bar and said, "See ya next time, Ben."

Out in the parking lot, the three of them sat in Tom's pickup truck.

"What the fuck happened to our pictures? I mean, I took a few, and none of them show the fish," Steve said.

Tom turned the key to start the truck and said, "I have no idea, but I had to get out of there because those guys were mocking us and looking at us like we were telling them we'd seen a UFO or something."

"Yeah, they sure were. And I'm sure they're still talking about us and our electric fish," Jeremy added with a laugh.

Tom chimed in. "Well, you both saw and felt what I did, right? I think we need to make it a point not to talk about this to anyone. It's only going to make us look like a bunch of crackpots, especially considering we couldn't produce a single picture of the fish. The last thing I need in this neck of the woods is a reputation. I'm up here almost every weekend, whereas you guys are only up a couple of times a year." It was clear he was trying to save face after the whole embarrassing bar incident.

"Hey, that's cool. As far as I'm concerned, it never happened, even though it did," Jeremy laughed.

"Same here. I get your concern, Tom. Makes sense. You don't want to be known as the tinfoil hat nutjob up here," Steve added.

Tom laughed at Steve's statement.

"But just remember it happened, and it was fuckin' weird, and it will have to remain our little secret," Tom said.

The other two nodded in agreement as Tom worked the speedometer up to sixty mph.

Beneath the hood, the motherboard of the truck's computer system began to exhibit early signs of a voltage overload.

Nightcall

The blinding light penetrated Christine's eyelids and woke her with a start. She blinked away the dream she'd been having only moments before, and her eyes slowly adjusted to the stark change in light. When she finally fixed her focus, she sat bolt upright in her bed. In the corner of her room, next to the dresser, stood a figure about a foot and a half tall. Its skin shimmered and shifted between aqua green and a brilliant orange. Next to the figure was an egg-shaped metallic orb hovering in mid-air. A ring of lights rimmed the lower third of the craft and circled it slowly in succession. The orb emitted no noise, nor gave any sense that it was idling or running. It simply held its place.

Christine fumbled for her glasses on the nightstand to bring the scene more clearly into focus. When she did, she could see the figure had abnormally large eyes and an oversized head, especially given its short stature. It had arms and legs much like humans, but both seemed comically thin compared to the rest of the being's torso.

Christine and her intruder were stuck in a momentary stare-down. She wondered if the being was dangerous or simply curious. After a brief period of complete silence, the being reared back and sneezed. A wad of alien snot shot out of the two holes that Christine assumed was its nose. It sat on her hardwood floor glowing fluorescent orange.

Christine instinctively said, "God bless you!"

The being tilted its large head to one side like a curious dog. "No, God bless you!" the being said. Its voice sounded electronic, like a bad automated phone system.

The being reached out and picked up the wad of glowing snot from the floor. It rubbed the goop into its skin at the abdomen, where it was absorbed, leaving no residue. "Excuse my expulsion. I think I picked up a nasty virus in the Aridani system. I've felt unwell for three light-years," it said.

"Wait, you speak English?" she said.

"It is one of my three million languages, yes. Well, three million plus a few if you consider the accent variations among the English-speaking countries. As beautiful as they are, the accents and language nuances we've seen in various parts of the world have no equivalent among the rest of the three million."

Christine laughed at the statement. "What are some examples?"

"Well, one of the best examples is right here in the Midwest. Terms like bubblers, hotdish, ope, ain'a hey, and uff da. What do they even mean? Then, there's Bostonians who say things like 'Ya can't pahk yah cah in the Hahvahd Yahd.' What? We've found these specific regional colloquialisms are unique to humans, especially in the English language. There's nothing wrong with them, but we find them amusing."

Christine laughed again. It was clear that this being was not only friendly but had a sense of humor to boot. Without provocation, the skin of the intruder turned a deep, warm blue. It struck Christine as being like a chameleon in the way it changed colors.

"So, what's with the color-changing thing?" she asked.

"It's a physiological response to what I am feeling. Each color equates to an emotional response."

"You're like a living mood ring! Well, I hope you don't perceive me as a threat."

"Yes, Christine, I have no fear of you based on the brain scan I did before your awakening. Your genetic makeup showed up with an 81% positive attribution. Not bad for a human. Most humans are way worse than eighty-one. I had a guy last week who scored a twenty-seven! Talk about a crappy person!"

Christine readjusted the covers up under her chin and laughed.

"How about your population? How do they score on this goodness scale?"

"Our race classifies entirely as 100% good. You must understand we are a highly developed population. Where we come from is twenty-seven generations into the future of your present day. It took all of those additional generations for our species to get to a state of 100% purified goodness."

Christine found the projection stupefying. The fact that humanity was twenty-seven generations away from genuine goodness was sobering. It gave her a sense of hopefulness, albeit a distant dream she'd never see.

"So, the world has nothing to fear from you? Is that what I'm hearing?"

"That is true. We are only interested in helping humans to stop destroying themselves and the amazing planet Earth."

The statement caused Christine to pause. She'd only ever thought about UFOs as spaceships with lasers capable of blasting cities out of existence. To dispel that perception and to consider them as friendly stretched her mind.

"What do you call your population, or species, or race— whatever you are?" Christine asked.

"Well, our technical name is GuptaClowns."

"Bahahaha! For real? You're called the *GuptaClowns*? You have got to be kidding." When the being did not respond, she followed up soberly with, "You *are* kidding, right?"

The GuptaClown's torso transitioned from deep blue into a shade of brilliant red.

"I hate to spoil your mirth, but no. That has been our name for millennia."

The two of them looked at each other awkwardly for a few moments before Christine broke the silence. "I'm sorry. I didn't mean to offend you. It's just that I was expecting a much more scientific name for your population. Something like Xanars or Plutanias or something. GuptaClowns just sort of caught me off guard, I guess."

The being's torso began a slow transition back to its comfortable blue, although of an unmistakably lighter shade. Christine assumed it was a change from blushing to a guarded sense of calm. Here she'd gone and practically insulted an entire superior species within the first ten minutes of meeting one of them.

"So, you've never really introduced yourself. I know you know my name, but what is yours?" Christine asked.

"Oh, so sorry. My name is Fred."

Christine struggled mightily to hold a straight face. Despite her efforts, the corners of her mouth raised slightly. She was talking to an alien known as a GuptaClown, whose name was actually Fred. *Nothing unusual here!*

"Well, then, hello, Fred. Does your kind have last names?"

"Yes, we do. Mine is Jaworski."

Oh my God, I can't even. Do not laugh. Do not laugh!

"So, Fred Jaworski. That is a great name. Do you have any Polish heritage?"

The being turned a brilliant shade of yellow and emitted a guttural burbling sound. It was an extended burble lasting nearly ten seconds. Christine stood smiling, wondering what was happening.

Fred spoke up, "Indirectly, yes. You see, GuptaClowns are all assigned the name of a human, living or dead, as part of their coming of age. The only requirement is that the human is or was good and kind-hearted. That said, there are very few names we take from the lives of politicians."

Christine grinned. "Well, that goes without saying, I think. Most are awful. So, what was Fred Jaworski famous for?"

"I never said famous; I said good and decent. There are plenty of famous people who are neither."

"Of course, my mistake. We humans like our idols," Christine said apologetically.

"Yes, GuptaClowns favor everyday, unsung heroes like Fred Jaworski. He grew up in Manitowoc, in the 1940s and was a gentle man, a good father, and a supportive spouse. He worked at the Marina for forty-one years and was a beloved coworker and friend to many. Mr. Jaworski also volunteered at the Manitowoc County Food Pantry and cared for his wife as she battled breast cancer for three years."

Christine nodded. "Interesting. Might I ask where your population came from? I mean, are you from the Milky Way Galaxy or somewhere else?"

Fred pressed a small button on the craft and activated the lid. The hatch flipped open with a woosh. Inside, Christine saw a simple cockpit. Attached to the armrest of the seat, there was a cupholder holding a Seven Eleven Big Gulp cup with a straw. Christine smiled at the irony of such technological wizardry alongside a plastic cup. The being reached into the craft, pulled out a tablet, and handed it to Christine.

"We are from a far distant galaxy you humans named JADES-GS-Z13-0. You can see it highlighted relative to your sun and planet on this display. Our official name for it is The Bronx."

"The Bronx? Haha! Oh my god, The Bronx! You're killing me here! Haha!"

"You humans are easily amused," Fred said.

Christine recognized her insensitivity. "Oh, there I go again. Sorry!"

Fred shrank to one-third of his normal size. He hung his head momentarily, then looked up at Christine again.

"Whoa, what just happened? Why did you shrink?" she asked.

"It's a long story, actually. Because we GuptaClowns are highly evolved, we are also highly sensitive. If we sense we are being laughed at, our stature diminishes. It's a sensitivity response. Usually, mockery and ridicule aren't an issue among our own. It's only when we are among humans that we seem to have this reaction."

Christine felt horrible. How could she have known that something as highly intelligent as an alien would have such intense sensitivity?

"I am so sorry. I laughed at the name of your galaxy. It's just that it matches the name of a popular borough in New York City, and I couldn't control my reaction to such a wild comparison."

Immediately, Fred returned to his normal size.

"Wait, there you go, changing size again. What's going on?"

"It seems your apologies are genuine and activated my self-esteem ingestors, which in turn fired up my synthesizers of growth and largesse that restored my stature."

"Remarkable. But might I ask why you didn't shrink when I laughed at the term GuptaClowns?" Christine asked.

"During our encounters, every human we have talked with has laughed at our name. We've developed our genetic code not to let that reaction bother us anymore. In the meantime, our fearless leader, Empress Lydia, is looking into renaming our race. We need a name that will not cause the human race to burst into laughter every time we say it."

"Well, to be honest, never in a zillion years would I have guessed one day an alien from 'The Bronx' would show up in my room claiming he was a representative of the GuptaClowns. In that respect, your leader is probably onto something," Christine said.

Fred nodded and stood there dumbly. An awkward silence elbowed its way into the conversation.

"Well, I should probably get back to sleep. I have to work in the morning. But I have one more question for you. What's with the Big Gulp in the cupholder there? Where'd you get that?"

"That? Oh, I got it at the 7-Eleven in Pewaukee about three years ago. It was during third shift when a clerk was out back smoking a cigarette. I slipped in and helped myself to a Grape Soda Gulp and kept the cup as a souvenir. It's the perfect reminder of American excess, indulgence, and its affection for nutritionally hollow junk food."

"Fair enough," Christine said.

"Well, I should be going. Bear in mind, I've seen to it that you will only have faint memories of this encounter in the morning," Fred said as he stepped into the craft.

"Wait, what?"

"Go Pack Go," Fred said as the lid closed. The ship quickly shrank and shot through the open window.

Through These Eyes

The ballgame was turning into a thriller. The Brewers and Cardinals were tied up 3-3 going into the eighth inning, and the crowd was getting revved up for what looked to be a nail-biting finish. Brendan was with his friends Jake and Mehul, who both shared his excitement at the prospect of a win, which would put the Brewers back into first place. They were in a three-team race with St. Louis and Chicago, so this was a pivotal game. Milwaukee won the first two of the series. A win today would sweep it and position them with momentum, approaching the playoffs.

"How many hits do the Brewers have, Jake? I can't read that scoreboard very well. Shit's all blurry," Brendan said.

"Really? You can't see those three-foot letters from here? Man, you've gotta get your eyes checked. Brewers have nine hits," Jake replied.

"Thanks for the lecture, Mom. I've been having a tough time seeing distance lately. I don't know what's up. Just getting old, I guess," Brendan said.

"Maybe, ya geezer. But seriously, that's nothing to mess around with. Just get them checked."

"I will. I am sixty-one, after all…" Brendan joked.

Brendan stared into the bright light of the ophthalmoscope as Dr. Soderberg peered at his eyeball from the other side.

Brendan always hated this part of the exam because it meant the doctor got uncomfortably close to his face as he conducted it.

"Hmmm..." the doctor said as he switched from the left eye to the right.

"What does hmmm mean?" Brendan asked.

After a few seconds, Dr. Soderberg pulled away and set the scope down on the counter. Brendon noticed a distinct change in the doctor's demeanor.

"Well, I'm afraid I've got some bad news. What I'm seeing looks like the initial stages of macular degeneration in both of your eyes. This affliction causes a loss of vision in the center of the eye. Over time, your vision will get blurrier, and it will get worse as you age. Unfortunately, it's not curable outside of some innovative research I've heard of."

"What? Are you kidding me? My grandmother had this, and she was essentially blind at the end. Are you telling me I have it, too?"

"Unfortunately, yes. I'm speculating, but there could be a genetic predisposition in your family history."

"That is not the news I wanted today. I noticed my vision was getting worse lately but just figured it was normal aging. Tell me more about the research you mentioned."

"Well, I hesitate to say too much because it is still so far out there, but there is a clinical study going on in California that purports to reverse the aging process in the human eye. It involves first a DNA scan of the patient, then a diagnosis and, if they are a suitable candidate, treatment."

"What does the treatment entail?" asked Brendan.

"From what I've read, it's a stem cell injection. Because it is still experimental, they are looking for ten people willing to take part in the study."

Brendan was intrigued by the prospect, but also suitably skeptical. He asked, "What are the downsides? Any negative side effects?"

"Again, from what I've read, it's too early to tell. That's what these clinical studies determine. The important thing is early detection. They've said the closer to diagnosis the patient gets treated, the higher the success rate."

"Hmmm. And the alternative without this treatment is steadily declining vision and eventual blindness?"

"I'm afraid so. I'll give you the name of the laboratory that is conducting the research, in case you want to pursue it. It's a proactive approach, obviously, but like I said, it's clinical research at this point," Doctor Soderberg reminded him. He scribbled down the name on a piece of paper and handed it to Brendan.

"Alright, Doctor, thanks for your honesty. I've got some thinking to do. I'll keep you posted."

Brendan sat across the table from his wife, Lynne, both of them nursing their second cup of coffee at a local shop. The place smelled of bakery, cinnamon, and espresso as alternative rock from the eighties and nineties spilled softly from the speakers overhead. They loved their Saturday routine, but this conversation had a seriousness about it.

"I think it's worth a shot, hun. I don't like the prospect of going blind a lot. This will affect you as much as me, so I want to make sure you're on board," Brendan said.

Lynne sipped her brew and set it on the table, cupping her hands around its warmth.

"Oh, I agree with you. I think it's something that needs to happen. I'm a little worried about what we don't know. Considering this is all so new, and the study only includes ten people. I just hope you don't do something you end up regretting."

"Well, whatever happens, it beats going blind," Brendan replied.

They both laughed uncomfortably. Brendan always had a great sense of humor, even if it was a bit dark at times. Lynne shared his ability to go to the dark places in search of some levity. This was one of those shared moments as they strove to see the future through an unclouded lens.

The waiting room at the clinic in San Francisco was empty except for one patient seated reading a magazine. Brendan and Lynne checked in at the registration desk and took a chair in the waiting area. After a ten-minute wait, a nurse came out and called his name. The two of them rose and followed the nurse back to a small conference room.

"The doctor will be with you in a few minutes. Thanks for waiting," she said.

"Thank you," Brendan replied.

Ten minutes later, the door opened, and a doctor came in. He was dark-haired and carried a small laptop.

"Mr. and Ms. Severson, I'm Doctor Drewe. Nice to meet you both."

"So, I've looked at your doctor's screening, and combined with your DNA scan, it looks like you are a perfect candidate for our study. You are early stage, under seventy years old, and in great health. I want to point out that this procedure is entirely new and untested, at least on humans. The results of studies conducted on animals have been extremely positive, which makes it attractive for clinical trials on humans. However, as I said, this is the first study of its kind, so it is impossible to predict the potential side effects. I will say it stands a high chance of reversing the macular degeneration that has already been done. This means at a minimum, you will see things better, possibly even better than you ever have. The downside is we don't know what we don't know. Typically, with these clinical studies, a small percentage of patients either don't respond well or don't respond at all to the treatment. When I say respond, I mean at least in relation to the results for the other participants. Make sense?"

Brendan hesitated and then began. "Yes, it does. I just want to let you know I am totally on board with this. It sounds so promising I'd be foolish not to take part."

"That is great. I will have them get you all the forms and set up a date for the procedure." He spent a minute typing on his laptop, filling in data about their meeting. He thanked Brendan, and as he turned to leave, he caught himself and spun on his heel.

"Oh, one other thing. In the months after the procedure, in addition to regular checkups, they will ask you to give monthly reports on what you're experiencing. Just routine stuff for a clinical."

"Sounds good, Doctor. Thanks again."

Dr. Drewe turned and left.

Brendan awoke groggily after the surgery. The hospital in San Francisco was well known for its ophthalmological care. The surgery was simple and brief, but Brendan requested sedation. It involved the injection of stem cells directly into the eyeball. He'd intentionally tuned out when the surgeon described the specifics, in part because of his weak stomach. He just wanted it done and laid his trust in his doctor.

When he woke, his eyes were covered with patches, but he overheard his doctor talking to Lynne. "He can take the patches off in two days, but I want him to take it easy for the next month or so. No air travel back home for two weeks, and remember, this is a new, experimental technique, so everyone will heal and react differently," the doctor said.

"Okay, Doctor. He and I can't thank you enough for accepting us into this trial. The thought of my husband going blind in his sixties was frightening to both of us. We are excited to see where this takes us."

"How long before I'll be back to normal?" Brendan asked.

"Well, as we talked about, if the cells regenerate as we hope, you should have most of your vision back in six months.

But, again, you are one of only ten people who have ever had anything like this done, so your mileage may vary," the doctor replied.

"That is good to hear. Thank you."

Lynne helped Brendan to his feet and, after signing the release paperwork, they took a taxi back to their hotel.

Brendan was so excited he could scream. It had been three weeks since his surgery, and his eyes seemed almost back to normal. He and Lynne were on their way to vacation to their favorite resort, a summer trip they both looked forward to every year. Brendan accelerated aggressively into the curve on Highway W in Vilas County. The Hyundai SUV whined and resisted throughout the bend. Like most SUVs, it was not a vehicle designed with racetrack-level performance in mind. It was a glorified grocery-getter, nothing more. Lynne turned her head toward him to see if he was paying attention. Brendan saw the glance but didn't respond.

The roadway returned to a straight, flat stretch, and Lynne went back to thumbing her phone. With hundreds of crystalline lakes and tall stands of pine, birch, and tamarack on both sides of the road, the drive was stunning. The majestic view wasn't enough to pull her attention fully away from the riveting appeal of the latest Facebook post, so phone time it was.

Upon seeing the curved arrow sign with a warning of 35 mph, Brendan felt a strange spark in his spirit. Instead of slowing, he adjusted his weight on the seat and punched the accelerator. The needle pushed fifty, then fifty-three as he again coaxed the Hyundai to corner in ways it was never intended.

"Brendan, what the hell are you doing? Slow down!" Lynne shrieked.

Brendan eased up on the accelerator and looked over at her. "Sorry. Heh, heh. I'm not sure what came over me. For a moment I felt like I was in my old Mustang."

"Well, that was twenty years ago, hun, and this sure isn't a Mustang, so stop it!"

Brendan gazed at the road and saw another sharp curve sign ahead. He fought the urge to speed up and also wondered where it had come from. The '78 Mustang from so many years ago was his idea, not Lynne's, a muscle car he'd bought from a friend as a second vehicle. It was a strange sort of testosterone status symbol. These curvy roads brought back memories of him pushing that car to its limits on trips around the state to show it off at car shows. His aggressiveness at the wheel had come out of nowhere, and it unnerved him a bit. He was sixty-one and was supposed to be driving like an adult. What was he thinking?

Post-operative health check: 30 days
Patient: Brendan Severson
Study ID: 202204069
Procedure: Macular Rejuvenation Trial

No major side effects to report. I feel great, and my vision is better already. I am seeing a little less of the cloudiness near the edge of my periphery. My distance vision is noticeably better. This surgery was the best decision ever!

The phone rang three times before Lynne finally picked up.

"Hi honey, it's me. I've only got a few minutes, but I wanted to ask you something."

"Okay, what is it?"

"Do you think we should try to have another baby? I mean, we're not getting any younger, and it seems like the right time of life to start again." The phone was silent for a full three seconds before Lynne finally reacted.

"What? Is this you, Brendan?"

"Yeah, it's me."

He waited, and after another pause, Lynne replied, "Have you been drinking?"

"No, honey. I'm at work and am totally serious. With Zach and Marissa out of the house, I feel like I'm thirty years younger. It would be fun to give them a sibling."

"Well, have you given any thought to the fact that you're sixty-one and I'm fifty-five? Remember that?" Lynne responded with a detectable edge of sarcasm.

"Yeah, but we can talk about it when I get home from work. I've been thinking, and I just don't want this part of our lives to pass us by."

"No, we can't talk about it tonight because there's nothing to talk about. That part of our lives *passed* us by and is done. Finished! It's just not going to happen. I'm not sure why you're even thinking something like this, but hopefully, you'll be over it by the time you get home. Now, I've got to run, but I'll see you tonight." Lynne hung up.

Brendan put his phone in his pocket. Even he wasn't sure where this urge to have another child had come from. He was just looking at the picture on his desk of him and his two kids in Myrtle Beach from twenty-five years ago and was overcome with nostalgia. It made him long for the days of reading to his kids, trips to the zoo, and taking them fishing. Despite his age, he felt a renewed need to bring another child into the world, a feeling he hadn't had since he and Lynne were in their thirties. He couldn't explain the urge in a way she would understand. Instead, he tried to put the thought out of his head and got on with his workday.

Post-operative health check: 90 days
Patient: Brendan Severson
Study ID: 202204069
Procedure: Macular Rejuvenation Trial

The cloudiness around the periphery of my eyes is 90% gone, I would guess. I have noticed a significant increase in energy and stamina. I don't know if it is related to the surgery, but I feel younger! It's probably just a temporary thing, or simply a desirable side effect of the procedure. All I know is I like it, and I feel great.

The following spring on a crisp afternoon, Brendan was enjoying the monthly outing with his friends, Jake and Mehul. Brendan sank the twenty-foot putt and pumped his fist victoriously. He bagged his putter and jumped in the cart. Mehul steered his way to the seventh hole, where the beverage cart was waiting. As they pulled up, Brendan couldn't help but notice the beverage girl, an attractive brunette. Sporting a pair of short shorts and a cute bob-cut, she was in her early twenties, less than a third his age. For some unknown reason, he found it difficult to take his eyes off her. He figured it was nothing more than a lecherous gawk, so he tried to hide it behind his sunglasses.

"Hi guys, does anyone need a beverage?" she asked.

"Yes, we do. We are so glad to see you. You're looking good today," Brendan said. The other guys gave him a look and an awkward laugh. Brendan didn't know where the comment came from but tried to laugh it off with the other guys. Still, he had a distinct sensation the girl was attracted to him, despite his gray hair and overweight paunch.

The cart girl blushed and asked, "What can I get you?"

"Well, your phone number for starters, then maybe an IPA," Brendan said.

"Dude, what?" Jake asked in disbelief. "You don't talk to the young lady like that!"

"Yeah, man. Not cool," Mehul added.

Brendan blushed a little, himself. *Where had that comment come from? I haven't come on to a girl in thirty years. But, dang, she is cute!* "Oh, I'm sorry, Miss. That was rude," Brendan apologized. Again, he wasn't sure where the thought had come from. It was like something was planted in his mind, and he had little control over it. He was acting like a twenty-something, to say nothing of the brazen, inappropriate message behind the statement.

The cart tender doled out their beers, took their tips, and motored away.

"What the hell was that, Brendan?" Mehul asked.

"You know, to be honest, I don't know where it came from. Although you have to admit she was good-looking."

"What? Just stop! She's younger than your daughter," Mehul countered.

"I know! That's why I can't explain why I said it. It's like I'm twenty-one again and I have no control over what I might say," Brendan pleaded.

"Well, if it keeps happening, you might want to seek professional help because it's way out of line, not to mention awkward," Mehul said with a serious look.

Brendan nodded, certifiably shamed by the entire incident. He had to agree that he'd been acting differently lately, outright weird at times. He couldn't help but think back to the tongue-lashing he'd taken from Lynne for suggesting that they try to have another child. It was like he had lost control over the speech filter in his brain. His behavior always seemed to be out of line for his age. It was something he definitely would have to monitor, as there was no way to explain it.

―――

Post-operative health check: 120 days
Patient: Brendan Severson
Study ID: 202204069
Procedure: Macular Rejuvenation Trial

Vision is almost 100%. As you know, per my visit to your office last week, I tested at 20/20. It's weird not needing glasses or cheaters anymore, but it sure makes life easier. It's like I'm thirty-five all over again! I even asked my wife if she wanted to have another child. I feel so young. She said I was crazy. Anyway, nothing else to report.

The shelves at the hobby store were lined floor to ceiling with boxes of model trains and slot car racing sets. Locomotives, rail cars, and tiny realistic scenes took up an entire section of the store. A large racetrack was set off to one corner where a couple of teens held controllers, as their respective Formula One model cars zipped around sharp curves at blazing speeds.

But none of those things appealed to Brendan. He was strictly there for the plastic models, more specifically, the cars from the seventies. Recently, he'd taken a new interest in model building. In his youth, it was an obsession of his before he grew out of it as a teen. For him, it was meditative, fitting the parts into one another with just the right amount of cement. He remembered listening to the hits of the seventies on his clock radio for hours as he built his tiny scale model cars.

The owner caught his eye as he walked in. "Can I help you, sir?"

"No, thank you. Just looking," Brendan replied. He chewed a wad of bubble gum, blowing and popping the occasional bubble as he made his way to the plastic model aisle. He scanned the boxes piled high on the shelves, looking for a specific '74 Gran Torino kit. The first model he built as a kid was a '74 Gran Torino, and he was eager to revisit the lines and assembly of it.

He found the model tucked between a Mustang and a Pontiac Firebird and, after sizing it up, slid it under his arm. He wandered to the end of the aisle to find a set of paints. Brendan was intent on using brush-on paint, not spray, much like he had when he was a kid. If he wanted to recreate the feel of what it was like, he'd stick with his old techniques. He grabbed a set of twelve colors, some paint thinner, and a tube of cement.

When he got to the counter, the clerk said, "Getting your grandson into the hobby?"

"Ha, ha. No, this is for me. I've decided I want to give it a go. I always enjoyed it as a kid, so I thought, what the heck?"

"Well, good for you, then. Can I interest you in some spray paint instead of this brush-on enamel stuff? It looks much more professional in the end."

"No. These are what I used years ago. They'll be fine."

"Suit yourself. No problem, my friend," the clerk said with a smile.

"Do you need to see my ID to buy the glue?" Brendan asked.

"Ha! No, I think you're good."

"Are you sure? I forgot to get a note from my mom," Brendan added in complete seriousness.

The clerk looked over his glasses at Brendan with a questioning glance. After Brendan failed to crack a smile, the clerk said, "Ah, no, sir. You're good. Just be careful with it, heh, heh."

"Oh, I will, sir. Thank you." Brendan was relieved he didn't have to prove his age. He wanted nothing to come between him and his new love of model cars. He walked out the door and couldn't wait to get home and set to work on it. Of course, Lynne thought it was odd, but she figured he was going through some late-in-life crisis where he was returning to his childhood pastimes to fill some hole in his life. And perhaps he was. He only knew it was something with which he was suddenly obsessed. Besides, everyone should have a hobby.

Post-operative health check: 180 days
Patient: Brendan Severson
Study ID: 202204069
Procedure: Macular Rejuvenation Trial

Vision continues to be very good. Even my close-up vision is better. I've taken up plastic model building and reading comic books. I don't even need to worry about putting on glasses to do either. My wife doesn't understand my new obsessions or the thought that being naked in front of her is terrifying to me, but I guess everyone is different in the world, right? (She thinks I need to go to therapy. Ha!)

Sweat dripped from Brendan's forehead, and his breathing was heavy as he walked down Delafield Street. He'd made great time on this run and was in cool-down mode. A month ago, he started running and was astonished by how it helped him expend some of his recently acquired energy. He typically walked the last half mile to bring his heart rate down and let the sweat dry.

A white panel van pulled over to the curb as he walked. The passenger, a middle-aged guy in a black polo shirt, rolled down the window. "Excuse me, kid. We're from Sugar Farm Enterprises, and we're doing a study on candy preferences. I'm wondering if you can help us out by trying some of our new products and letting us know what you think?"

If there was one weakness Brendan had fought with his whole life, it was his sweet tooth. He loved cookies, candy, and soda and had a mouthful of cavities to prove it. This offer sounded like a dream come true.

"Sure thing, mister," he said.

"Great, I'll show you what we've got."

The passenger climbed out and opened the sliding side door. Brendan could hardly believe his eyes. There were open boxes of candy bars, licorice, taffy, and other sweet treats. Brendan's eyes almost bugged out of his head. He walked over to get a closer look.

"I can have any of these I want?" he asked the man in the polo shirt.

"Sure can, kid. Take what you like, and we'll give you a survey to take home, fill out, and mail back to us."

"Sweet deal!" Brendan surveyed the products, hypnotized by the allure that lay before him. As he reached for the chocolate Bango Bar, he felt a sharp blow to his skull, and everything went black.

The courtroom was packed with spectators. In front of the judge's bench sat the plaintiff's attorney, Brendan, and his wife. The adjacent table held two attorneys in gray, expensive suits and wingtips.

The prosecuting attorney stood to present his closing argument.

"Your Honor and to the jury, I think the evidence and facts we've heard speak for themselves. The testimonies of the witnesses have proven that Visioneers Plus has committed several serious egregious offenses over the last two years. It's clear they were negligent in conducting the proper testing of their macular rejuvenation solution prior to its use on human subjects. They desperately tried to cover up the fact that the procedure affected the human brain, causing psychological age regression in the clinical participants, resulting in irreparable pain and suffering for them, their families, and friends. This includes job loss, loss of income, and thousands of dollars in medical bills spent trying to figure out what was happening to Mr. Severson."

The prosecuting attorney took a small sip from his water bottle and continued. "Of course, all of this is compounded by the manner in which Visioneers Plus covered up the problem, namely by assaulting and kidnapping Mr. Severson and holding him at a facility in the remote town of Little Lake, Michigan. It was here that he was discovered by some curious locals being held against his will. In light of all these charges, I trust the jury will choose to rule in the way of justice, allowing Ms. Severson to recover a sense of financial security in her life, care for her husband, and put this corporation out of business forever."

The attorney returned to his seat next to his assistant. Seated to her right was Brendan, who was inattentively engrossed in the horse he was working on in his coloring book near a sippy cup holding his apple juice.

Acknowledgments

Gratefully acknowledged are the following publications, where portions of this book appeared in earlier forms:

Portage Magazine, Raw Earth Ink, Syncopation Literary Journal, Creative Wisconsin Magazine, The Paradox Magazine, Lakefly Writing Contest 1st Place, A Stitch in Time Anthology, See Me Anthology.

I'd like to thank a few folks who made this book possible. First and foremost, to my wife, Donna, a stalwart supporter of my work. She's brutally aware that living with a creative poses its challenges, but also fully recognizes my need to write. I love you forever. I am grateful to my friend and writing colleague, Greg Peck, for his editorial assistance. Thanks also to the women writers of my Wisconsin Writers Association critique group and those of my Café De Arts critique group for their feedback on some of these stories.

Thanks to my friend, Pat Judd, for his unending support and for believing in me back in the eighties, way before I did. And deep gratitude to all those colleagues who took the time to read my work before publishing and provide a blurb, including Frank Bures, Nick Chiarkas, Steve Fox, Robert Goswitz, Nancy Jorgensen, Nancy Rathbun, and Greg Renz.

I'm also eternally grateful to the people of Wisconsin, Minnesota, and surrounding states who call the Midwest their home. Their warmth, practicality, and quirkiness inspired these stories, and I can't imagine a better place to grow up and call my home.

To the director and publisher of Cornerstone Press, Dr. Ross Tangedal, thank you for again believing in me and supporting me as I cross over into the world of fiction for the first time. Thanks also to the team at Cornerstone, including my editor, Ellie Atkinson, and her editorial assistants, including Eleanor Belcher, Christina Niedzwiecki, Asher Schroeder, and the rest of the Cornerstone staff. The community at Cornerstone Press feels like a family, and I'm thankful for the working relationship we've cultivated.

JIM LANDWEHR is the author of four memoirs: *At the Lake* (Cornerstone Press 2022), *Cretin Boy*, *Dirty Shirt*, and *The Portland House*. He also has six published poetry collections: *Tea in the Pacific Northwest*, *Thoughts from a Line at the DMV*, *Genetically Speaking*, *Reciting from Memory*, *Written Life*, and *On a Road*. His nonfiction has been published in *Main Street Rag*, *The Sun Magazine*, *Story News*, and others. His poetry has been featured in many journals and magazines. Jim is a board member of the Wisconsin Writers Association and the Wisconsin Fellowship of Poets. He is retired and enjoys traveling, fishing, kayaking, biking, and all things outdoors. He was the 2018–2019 poet laureate for the Village of Wales, Wisconsin.

For more on his writing, visit: jimlandwehr.com

www.ingramcontent.com/pod-product-compliance
Lightning Source LLC
LaVergne TN
LVHW040058080526
838202LV00045B/3690